I AM THE SHADOWMAN

And Other Supernatural Tales

PATRICIA HOPKINS

I Am The Shadowman (And Other Supernatural Tales)

Edited by Paul Alexander Rancier

Published in the United States by Wanderlust Books

Cover art photo Shutterstock / 34317073 / Bob Orsillo

ISBN-10: 098576130X
ISBN-13: 978-0-9857613-0-1

Also written by Patricia Hopkins

More Than A Notion

For Anthony and Zachary

Mi rey te amo.

TABLE OF CONTENTS

I AM THE SHADOWMAN

PROLOGUE

I was only fourteen when I killed my first *Shadowman*. After the first kill, it became easy. Mother always said killing was in my blood and the more I practiced, the better I would be at it. She was right.

My best friend and I were out doing what fourteen year old girls do—shopping for clothes. After leaving the shopping mall laden down with shopping bags, we came upon a man attacking a small child. My friend and I ran up to them, yelling and screaming for the man to leave the child alone. We were just a few feet from the struggle when I saw the man up close. When he turned to face us, that's when I first saw it. The momentary flash of darkness behind the man's eyes gave him away. *My first real Shadowman!*

He scurried off into a dark alley with the two of us at his heels. While running to keep track of the creature, I looked over my shoulder to check on its victim. The young girl we rescued lay balled up in a heap in the middle of the parking lot, loudly thanking us for scaring away the crazed man. From all outward appearances, we were just two teenage girls out shopping, so he never expected it would be us who would finally take him down. After two years of practicing for my first kill, the time had finally come to make good use of my training.

We cornered the Shadowman against the alley wall. He pleaded for his pathetic life and tried to make us believe it was something other than what it was. Then it growled and cursed us to hell. My friend immobilized the thing with the fine mist issued by the Agency—trapping the dark spirit in its mortal shell. I narrowed my eyes and wielded the long knife I kept hidden in my backpack in one swift motion across his thick neck. An oily dark substance resembling congealed blood oozed from his wounds. The Shadowman tried in vain to escape but it was trapped in the man's dying body. It shrieked in agony as if the screams came straight from hell.

My friend was on the verge of becoming hysterical over our deed. Not me. I remember standing there not feeling a thing as I watched the life seep from the Shadowman's body—not even a shred of sympathy for the man it overtook. What I did know was in less than an hour, the rapid decomposition process would leave nothing but dust. I shot my fist upwards in victory. *My first kill! And I was on top of the world!*

CHAPTER ONE

Supernatural forces known as Shadowmen have existed since the beginning of time—before the dawn of creation. They come from the bowels of hell and have roamed the earth in search of human hosts ever since. Able to hide in plain sight, these spirits blend in with the shadows of our everyday lives and live on the fringe of our existence. Every now and then you may catch a glimpse of one from the corner of your eye, slinking across a wall or down a flight of stairs. To maintain a grasp on our sanity, we dismiss the sightings as a figment of our imagination.

Shadowmen prowl the earth in search of an opportunity—any opportunity to win over innocent souls. They prey upon individuals who possess the slightest proclivity towards embracing evil. These spirits insidiously work their way inside a person and slowly take over, killing off any remaining hint of decency. Once they get inside, there is no way out other than death. And even that is no guarantee. Most people invite these dark evil spirits in by their behavioral choices—others do so intentionally. The result becomes the most evil, hateful, destructive people one can imagine. Left unchecked the Shadowmen will destroy the earth and all who reside on it. Seems lately, they're winning.

I waited patiently in the service department of the used car dealership to speak to the salesman about my warranty. As I listened to the man speak, I suspected he could be a Shadowman because of the obvious disdain displayed towards his customers. Nothing about the man was extraordinary. He stood about six feet tall, of average build, and overall was an attractive middle aged black man. What gave him away was his attitude. In most cases, it always does.

"Sir, everybody knows you can't return an item after the warranty has expired. What are you, dense?" He smirked then laughed.

The old man started to speak, but changed his mind when he noticed the salesman shoving his paperwork back inside the envelope.

"So you expect me to give you your money back? Really?! You people are always trying to get something for nothing," he uttered under his breath in a dismissive condescending tone.

"There's no need to be nasty about it," replied the elderly black man. "The only reason you know so much about extended warranties is because you sell these worthless pieces of crap to unsuspecting people for a living. You're nothing more than a glorified used car salesman!" he replied, with disgust in his voice. The man grabbed his hat and stood to leave.

And that's when I saw the Shadowman make his brief appearance. The salesman's eyes went dark as a moonless sky on a Halloween night. If I had blinked, I would have missed it. He almost had me fooled with his fast talking and his slick demeanor. Almost, but not quite.

My hand instinctively clamped down tightly around the small sleek canister hidden in my purse. My index finger was poised to spray at a moment's notice. I watched the salesman's mouth move as he sat behind the desk with an infuriatingly smug expression stamped across his face. Dressed fashionably in dark slacks, a white dress shirt with gold cuff links, and expensive designer suspenders, he gave off the impression he was more successful than he was.

Years ago, the Agency had perfected the mist so Seers no longer need to physically slaughter Shadowmen in order to destroy them. The mist worked effectively by causing a metabolic breakdown in the blood cells of Shadowman. Once asleep or unconscious, the mist's effects trapped the Shadowman's spirit inside the host and quickly caused the body to decompose. After all was said and done, only dust remained. Funny thing was no one ever reported missing a loved one because once the Shadowman took hold, most people were happy to have that person out of their life.

The salesman regained his composure and said, "Well, I'm sorry you feel that way, but you're still not getting your money back." The salesman dismissed the elderly couple with a wave of his hand and returned to whatever he was doing.

I observed the raw emotion on the old man's face. He reached for his wife's hand. She smoothed down her dress and used her cane to stand. They walked out the dealership, deflated and defeated. The couple reminded me of my grandparents. I was pissed off anyone could treat such a nice old couple so badly.

The salesman looked up when he noticed me standing in his doorway. He pursed his lips and asked, "What do…I mean, can I help you?"

"I know who you are. I know what you are. But you don't know who I am. Now you will." I pulled the canister from the inside pocket and sprayed the fine mist directly in his face. He gasped, coughed, and yelled out, "What the hell is wrong with you?! Get the hell out of my office! Security!"

I held my car's warranty documents tightly to my chest and quickly fled the dealership, making sure I left nothing behind. Although I was very cautious to never reveal my true identity, one could never be too careful. I was extremely good at what I did, but all it would take was one minor slip up and my secret would be out.

By dawn, the salesman would be dead and gone—never to be seen nor heard from again. *Wish I could be there to witness that asshole turn to dust. I'd be more than happy to flush his ashes down the toilet!* I never worried about the effects of the mist on humans. For regular folks, the mist was as harmless as distilled water.

* * *

Back in the day, my parents described me as a precocious child due to my very curious nature. I incessantly questioned everything and everybody, no matter the situation. They thought I was just being inquisitive. However, most other adults just called me a pain in the ass. I was also "different". My mother was advised on more than one occasion to have me checked out by a professional because I didn't act like most girls. Where other girls my age were fascinated by boys, my interest resided in reading books about the paranormal or supernatural.

Miss Jergens, my middle school guidance counselor, first introduced me to the Agency when I was twelve, because I spent most of the sixth grade sitting in her office doing homework. None of the teachers could deal with me and no one wanted me in their classroom. They said I was disruptive to the class and a bad influence on the other children. I couldn't help it, I was bored.

One day I was helping Miss Jergens move boxes of old books into the storage room. It was dark and the light was burned out. The darkness never bothered me, for my night vision was as sharp as it was in the daylight.

She flipped the switch but nothing happened. "Aria, place the box in the hallway. Let's wait until we get the light bulb replaced. I don't want you falling down and getting hurt," she said.

"What do you mean? I can see fine." My vision automatically adjusted to gather together tiny particles of light to brighten the room.

"Impossible! Its pitch black in there!" she replied.

I continued towards the back of the storage room and placed the box in the corner with the rest of the old books. "No it's not. I found the stack with no problem. What's the matter?" I asked.

"Come here," she instructed. "Let me see your eyes." She peered closely at my eyes. Her hand reflexively went to her mouth to cover a gasp of surprise.

"What's wrong Miss Jergens?" Her reaction frightened me.

"Your eyes… You have the eyes of a *Seer*—a gatherer of light," she responded. "You should be with them—your own kind. I must let them know I have found you."

Grabbing my arm, she hurried back to her office, shut the door, and made a phone call to a mysterious party. I didn't hear the conversation, but I understood it was about me. Wondering what the fuss was about, I looked at my eyes in a mirror and saw nothing out of the ordinary. However, my eyes always were extremely sensitive to light.

She opened the door and simply stated, "I'm going to recommend you for this school. It's a special school for children who are extraordinarily gifted. Give your parents this card and tell them what I said. As of today, you are no longer enrolled in this school."

That was the last time I heard from Miss Jergens. She was probably happy to have me out of her overly relaxed, bleached blonde hair. I was a handful even for her.

So, it was during the summer before seventh grade when I learned the roles and responsibilities of being a Seer. Due to their unique ability to see in extremely low levels of light and their talent for detecting the presence of evil, Seers are able to locate Shadowmen who hide within unsuspecting people. Seers maintained constant watch over Shadowmen with the primary mission being to destroy them all. For once Shadowmen ceased to exist, the world would once again be safe. Also, according to the elder Seers, only certain individuals were born with the power to destroy the Shadowmen. I was one of the lucky. Or so I thought.

CHAPTER TWO

After fifteen years of slaying Shadowmen, killing became routine—a sport. Considering my earlier kills, I preferred the physical aspect of feeling a Shadowman's life slip away, more so than the "humane" misting of the creatures. The mist was clean, simple, and quick acting and caused the human body to feel no pain while effectively getting rid of the Shadowman. The Agency preferred the latter to prevent Seers from sliding down the slippery slope of *doing evil to prevent evil*. Even so, I wanted to get my hands dirty like I used to. Consequently, after years of ridding the world of evil, I soon discovered my thirst for killing Shadowmen could not be satisfied.

Because misting took no physical skill or special abilities, it became much too easy. So to ward off boredom, several of us Seers competed to see how many Shadowmen we could kill in a week. We turned it into a competition and an inexpensive meal at McDonald's became the prize. However, due to my insatiable appetite for killing and wanting to feel the death of the Shadowman at my fingertips, for me the reward wasn't the meal, but the actual killing itself. Thus, as a result of my extremely competitive nature, I was rewarded with a Big Mac meal every weekend for five years straight. No other Seer ever came close to breaking my record.

Other than being a Seer and slayer of Shadowman, my life was fairly normal. In fact, I loved my life. I loved my husband. But I loved killing Shadowman even more. I thought about earlier. What I didn't love was having to go back to the dealership and dealing with another asshole over this warranty. *I should've taken care of my warranty before I misted that jerk!* I thought, while I drove home. I parked my car in the garage next to my husband's and went inside.

"Hey sweetheart, how you doing today?" asked Elijah, my husband of three years. He was also a Seer.

"I've been feeling a bit tired lately and I can't keep anything down. I think I'm catching the flu or something." I pulled my long dreads into a ponytail holder and tossed my bag onto the floor.

Elijah touched his hand to my forehead, "You don't feel warm. Why don't you make an appointment with the doctor? It's probably a good idea to get checked out just to make sure you're alright."

"I suppose so... You know how much I hate going to the doctor." I opened the refrigerator and pulled out a cold slice of pizza.

"Baby please go get checked out. You never get sick." He encircled me with his arms. "I've noticed you're picking up a little weight too."

"Boy, get outta here! I am not pregnant! Don't even start that mess!" I counted backwards to my last cycle and couldn't remember when the last one was.

"Sure would be nice to have a little Aria running around here." He kissed my neck.

"What happens if it's a boy? Oh shoot! What am I saying?! I am not pregnant!"

Elijah returned to his place on the sofa, only this time with a beer in hand. "So what exciting things did you do today?" he asked.

"Just the usual stuff. Eliminated a few Shadowmen. Nothing spectacular," I replied.

"Aria, you are the only Seer I know who can be so nonchalant about killing. We all know how evil they are and why we must get rid of them, but you make it sound like you're brushing your teeth."

"I'm just better at disassociating myself. I learned that trick when I was a kid, to not let stuff get to me. It's no big deal. They were only Shadowmen. Nobody is going to cry over their deaths." I took a sip of his beer.

"Hey, hey, hey, give me that. Until you find out whether you're pregnant or not, no more alcohol for you."

"Whatever! You're just jealous I've been number one Seer for five years straight. I am the queen slayer of Shadowmen!" I boasted and danced around the room pretending to be Muhammad Ali.

"I'm just saying that it's not normal to feel nothing when you kill someone. Shadowman or not. Now come here and give me some loving, woman!"

Early the next morning, the doctor advised me to come in for an exam right away, especially since I couldn't remember having my last period. I sat on the examination table wearing nothing but a paper gown for at least twenty minutes in a cold sterile room. How many times can you read the same poster explaining how your body changes during each trimester? I found out. At least fifty.

The door opened and the nurse pushed back the thin drape encircling the examining table. "Good news Mrs. Griffin, you're pregnant!" replied the nurse with a big grin.

The unexpected news put me into a state of shock and I was unable to provide an intelligible response. Being pregnant had never entered my mind so I idiotically muttered, "Huh?"

"Congratulations!" You're about ten weeks pregnant!

The nurse proceeded to give me a laundry list of things I needed to take care of. She went over foods I should avoid, told me no more alcohol or tobacco. Gave me a prescription for huge prenatal vitamins that I was supposed to choke down every morning.

I walked out of the office in a daze. I thought, *Me pregnant? What am I going to do with a baby?* I was so distracted from the news that when I saw a Shadowman lurking behind the eyes of the pharmacist, I let it go. *I never let it go! How am I going to continue being a Seer with a baby in tow?*

I picked up the cell phone to call Elijah. The phone vibrated in my hand. It was him.

"So what did the doctor say?" Elijah asked.

"You were right. I'm pregnant." I answered.

"Baby, that's great. Are you excited?"

"Not yet, I'm still in shock. Baby, how am I going to work? I won't be able to function as a Seer."

"Forget about being a Seer! And about the Shadowman for a minute! There are plenty of Seers around to cover you. It's not going to be forever. Damn it Aria! This is our child for God's sake!"

"You're right, Elijah. This is our baby. I am going to be a mother." For my husband's sake, I tried to channel his excitement.

"There you go. Now go on home and we'll celebrate after I get off work," he said.

"Alright, I'll see you at home. I love you!"

My throat felt like it was filled with sand. I was thirsty and needed something to drink so I drove to the nearest convenience store to buy a bottle of water.

The store was empty except for the cashier and a lone customer in the back. The customer, a man in his mid to late forties, was milling around the beer cooler speaking to himself, or perhaps he wore an earpiece and was on the phone. He looked like an engineer or an accountant because of the manner in which he was dressed. He wore a plain white shirt, accented by the prerequisite pocket protector, and dark khaki pants. *I got it!* I thought, *he reminds me of Michael Douglas in that movie about a guy who snaps and goes on a crime rampage in downtown Los Angeles.*

Grabbing a bottle of water from the cooler, I unintentionally glanced in his direction. That is when I saw what he was. The darkness of his soul was revealed in those eyes—eyes so dark you couldn't even see the whites. He was a full-blown Shadowman who no longer felt the need to hide.

I reached inside my purse and felt around for the mist. I couldn't let this one get away. Full-blown Shadowmen were worth two of the regular ones. *Extra points for one kill!* I was excited. He walked towards the cashier and threw his money on the counter.

"Sir, I need another $1.25," said the cashier.

"I ain't got no more cash on me," replied the man, returning his wallet to his back pocket.

"Well then you can't buy this beer, sir." The cashier tried to place the beer behind the counter.

The man growled at the kid and said, "I said I ain't got no more money and I'm taking this beer. You wanna try and stop me?! Come on!"

"Sir, I'm just trying to do my job. I can't sell you this beer until you pay me the rest of the money."

Sizing up the situation, I knew this was about to go south really fast. The kid had no idea what he was messing with. I walked up to the counter and tossed a couple of dollars on the counter.

The man looked directly at me, grabbed his beer, and walked out the door without saying a word.

He was almost at his car! I was about to lose my opportunity to get the Shadowman so I called out, "Excuse me sir, you forgot something!" I rushed out the door after him.

He turned around and looked at me with those funky black eyes. "What did I forget bitch?" he snarled.

My heart pounded a thousand beats a minute. I pulled out the can and squirted the mist directly in his face. He didn't flinch a muscle. I squirted him again. He wiped his face with one hand, grabbed my arm with the other, and pushed me backwards into the wall. He jumped in his car and calmly drove away.

Realizing what I'd just done, I started to hyperventilate. The quick shallow breaths caused me to develop tunnel vision, so I eased down to the sidewalk to ward off the impending fainting spell. The cashier rushed outside.

"Miss, are you alright? You want your water?" He pressed the cool wet bottle to my forehead.

"Thanks, I'm okay now. I got a bit dizzy. I'm fine, really." *Oh shit!* I thought. I had broken the cardinal rule for Seers. Never under any circumstances, let a Shadowman touch you— especially a fully developed Shadowman. I looked at my wrist. An ugly bruise was starting to form. I tried rubbing the hot area to relieve the pain, then took the remaining water and poured it on my wrist.

"That dude was crazy! I'm glad you jumped in when you did," replied the cashier. He looked at me again. "You sure you're alright? You don't look too good."

"I just need to get to my car. I'm fine." I managed to stand and tried shaking off the heavy curtain of weariness that threatened to overcome me. I got in my car and headed home.

* * *

"Baby? Baby, wake up! Aria, are you alright?" asked Elijah with concern.

"Huh, what's going on? What are you doing home already?" I asked, yawning sleepily.

"I've been trying to get in touch with you all day. I've been calling your cell phone and the house phone for hours. You didn't return any of my calls or answer my texts. I was worried sick."

"Dang honey, I just came home to take a quick nap after my doctor's appointment this morning. What are you tripping for?" I pushed myself up in the bed.

"Aria, it's after seven. What time did you get home?"

I looked at the clock on the nightstand and sat up. "It's seven o'clock?! Oh my God! I got home around ten thirty this morning. There is no way I could have slept the entire time!"

He touched my forehead. "You're burning up. I'll bring you a glass of water."

Elijah was right. I was hot and my wrist hurt. There was a deep purple bruise where the Shadowman grabbed me. Something was wrong.

"Here you are. Drink this and take these aspirin. We need to get your temperature down."

I popped the two white tablets into my mouth and drank the full glass of water in one gulp. "Thanks."

"That should make you feel better. So what did the doctor say this morning?"

"Like I told you earlier, I'm pregnant. Already two and a half months!" I rubbed my tummy, looked up at my lovable husband and smiled. Finally, I felt as excited as he. "Elijah, we're going to have a baby! Can you believe it?!"

He placed his hands over mine and said, "I love you. Wow! I'm going to be a Dad!"

The waves of nausea hit me out of nowhere. I bolted from my bed and ran into the bathroom. But there was nothing to throw up because I hadn't eaten all day. It must have been the water.

"Aria, I think you may need to go back to the doctor. I'm worried about you." He joined me in the bathroom. "Hey what happened to your wrist?"

"Oh that," I stopped to wipe my mouth with a dry towel. "You'll never guess who I ran into earlier today. Go ahead, guess."

Elijah shrugged. "I don't know. Who?"

"I came across a full-blown Shadowman! He didn't have any whites left in his eyes at all!" I replied excitedly. "It took two squirts of the mist to stop him."

"I'm impressed! We Seers don't come across their kind very often." Elijah gave me a high five. "Congratulations on taking him down! Sometimes it takes two or three Seers at once to get a full Shadowman. So how'd you do it?"

I sat on the side of the bathtub and nonchalantly explained, "I paid for his beer, then followed him out of the store and misted him. When the first hit didn't get a reaction, I squirted him again. Elijah, this'll really help my numbers because fully developed Shadowmen are the most difficult to destroy."

"I wish you would stop being so concerned with your numbers! You could've been hurt, Aria." He nervously ran his hands over my arm. "You actually faced off with that thing? Stood up to a full Shadowman on your own?!"

"Yes, I did. You *do* realize they're worth two regular kills in the competition! Anyway, now I understand why it would take a couple of Seer's to take them down. They're pretty strong," I said rubbing my wrist.

"Wait a minute Aria, you mean to tell me you're concerned about your numbers at a time like this?! Did that thing do *this* to you?" Elijah looked alarmed.

"It's nothing. Just a little bruise. It'll go away in no time." I hoped. I didn't know what the ramification of being touched by a full blown creature was, but it couldn't be good.

Elijah stood and started pacing the floor. "Get dressed, we're leaving right now! I've got to get you to the Agency."

"Honey, what's wrong?" I asked. He frightened me because nothing ever upset Elijah. This time he looked really worried. No, he looked positively scared.

"Aria, we don't have time to talk. I need to get you to the Agency."

"Fuck you! I'm not going anywhere! Motherfucka!" I heard the words come out of my mouth, but they were not my own.

Elijah stopped dead in his tracks. He looked deeply into my eyes—examined them, and breathed a sigh of relief.

I covered my mouth with both hands because I had never spoken to Elijah like that. I would never say those vile words to him. Not to the love of my life.

He searched through my closet, found what he was looking for and tossed me a pair of sweats. "Let's go...."

The Agency resided in a non-descript concrete building resembling a WWII bunker. From the outside, one would have no idea what went on inside. Elijah buzzed the ringer on the front door.

"Identify yourself." Came a voice from inside a speaker mounted outside the main door.

"Elijah and Aria Griffin to see Doctor Watts," he replied.

"Please look into the retinal scanner," instructed the voice.

Elijah did as he was told and placed his chin on the device. An ultraviolet light beam passed quickly across his pupils, highlighting the retina to make sure he was authorized to proceed.

"You're clear, sir. Mrs. Griffin, your turn."

I followed Elijah's movements and rested my chin on the holder. The beam of light passed across my eyes once, then passed by once more. I stood anticipating the all clear notification.

"One more time, ma'am, there seems to be a problem with the scanner. It has never acted like this before. Let's try one more time," the guard instructed.

Both Elijah and I knew what the problem was. The Shadowman had probably made a brief appearance just as the ultraviolet beam crossed my retina. I took a deep breath and again placed my chin in the scanner's chin rest.

"I'm ready." I prayed the Shadowman would remain dormant for a few more minutes. I held my breath and tried not to blink as the bright light scanned my eyeball. I imagined the guard would send a laser beam into my skull if he were to find out I was exposed to the Shadowman's touch. I visualized my head exploding into a million tiny pieces as my poor husband looked on.

"That's better. Probably just a hiccup in the system. You're clear ma'am."

The door opened and we went inside. Several years had passed since I last visited the Agency. The most recent time was when Elijah and I got married. Because Seers could only marry certain people, the potential spouse had to be checked out beforehand by a Supreme Seer. When it came to love, Seers weren't able to detect the devious Shadowmen who lurked within their mates. Therefore a Supreme Seer was required to verify that the person was free of a Shadowman's influence before he would provide his approval of their union.

We were led to a sterile white waiting room. The receptionist sat behind a plexiglas wall, busily pecking on a keyboard. She looked up and smiled acknowledging our presence, then returned her attention to her task.

"Elijah, tell me what's going on please. Why are we here? And why are you acting so strangely?"

"I'm frightened for you my love. For us and our baby. When you told me that creature actually put his hands on you... Well, I know from stories shared by other Seers that nothing good ever comes from being touched by one of those things." He sat back and rubbed his face.

"What do you mean? I'm a Seer. He can't hurt me. Can he?"

"I don't know. That's why I wanted to see the doctor. Let him examine you and make sure you're okay. I love you and I don't want anything bad to happen to you."

I sat back and thought about my predicament. In one short day, I discovered I was carrying my first child, yet my happiness may have been destroyed all because of my need to get another kill. *Perhaps my thirst for blood has finally caught up with me,* I thought.

"Aria Griffin?" asked the man in a white coat standing in the doorway.

"I'm Aria," I replied.

"Ma'am, please follow me. The doctor is waiting."

"Can my husband also come?" I needed Elijah to be with me.

"I'll get him after the doctor does the examination. He can wait here for now," replied the man.

"Go on, I'll be fine." Elijah tried to put on a happy face.

I reluctantly followed the man through the door and into an examination room. He never identified himself so I assumed he was a nurse. At least this room was warm and inviting, unlike the cold sterile room from earlier in the day. I took a seat in one of the comfortable recliners and picked up an old magazine to leaf through while I waited, trying to calm myself.

The doctor knocked before he came in. I almost laughed when I saw a slightly older version of Doogie Howser enter the room. This kid looked like he wasn't even out of puberty.

"Aria Griffin?" he asked and extended his hand. "Hi, I'm Doctor Watts."

I almost laughed but contained the urge. "Nice to meet you, doctor."

He took a seat opposite mine and said, "I know you're probably wondering what this kid is doing here? Right?" He looked amused.

I shook my head. Although that *was* what I was wondering.

"Don't be embarrassed. It's what all patients think the first time they meet me. Well first of all, I am not as young as I look. I have a hormone problem which keeps me from aging at the same rate as most people. While I appear to be fifteen, I am actually thirty-one." He browsed through my chart.

"Wow!" I uttered. I realized how stupid my response was, but it was appropriate.

He took my response in stride and got on with it. "Let's see. You were first identified as a Seer at the age of twelve. During school you were extremely gifted—graduating at the top of your class. Very good! And you have an impressive number of kills. Hmm, all-in-all, it appears you have done very well as a Seer. Now what brings you here today?"

"Um, well, I just found out I was pregnant this morning…"

"Congratulations. Your first?" he asked.

"Yes, it's our first," I replied and exhaled.

He took notes in my chart as I spoke. "Go on, I'm listening."

"After after my doctor's appointment this morning, I was thirsty so I stopped off at a convenience store to purchase a bottle of water.

"Um hum…" He nodded, studying me.

"While I was getting my water, I noticed a full blown Shadowman in the store. He was giving the store clerk a hard time. I intervened so I could get a closer look and because I didn't want to let him get away. I followed him outside the store and misted him. Well, the first shot didn't have any effect, so I misted him again.

Spraying him twice really pissed it off. The man grabbed me by my wrist and pushed me away—against the wall. Then he drove off. That's it."

"He, I mean, *it* actually touched you?" The doctor became concerned. Alarmed.

"Only my wrist. When I told Elijah, he freaked and said he needed to get me here. To see you. So really I don't know why I'm here."

"Give me your wrist," he instructed.

I put out my wrist and let him exam it. He looked at it from all different angles. Then he pulled a silver canister and misted my arm. Immediately, the skin became inflamed.

"Ouch, that stings! What's going on doctor? Am I going to be alright?" I pulled back my arm and rubbed the burning, itching area.

"Aria, how have you been feeling lately? In regards to being a Seer?"

"What do you mean? I feel fine."

"I see you have a record number of kills. In fact, you seem to have an extraordinary number under your belt. Tell me, how do you feel when you kill a Shadowman? Do you experience any signs of guilt, remorse, sadness? Is this affecting your life in a negative way? Have you ever felt you wanted to stop doing this?"

"To tell you the truth doctor, I love killing Shadowman. In fact, I seek them out. I challenge myself to get as many a day as I can. When I saw the full fledged creature, I couldn't let him get away. And no, I don't feel any remorse. Killing gives me a thrill. A high like nothing else does." The look of concern on his face made me pause. "Why do you ask?"

He sat back and studied me without saying a word. He then shook his head and let out a deep, long sigh. "That is what I was afraid of. Most Seers are unable to kill without feeling some kind of emotion. Some bit of empathy for the human part not taken over by the Shadowman. Your getting so much pleasure from killing is quite troubling."

"Troubling? Why? Isn't that what we're supposed to be doing? Ridding the earth of the evil Shadowmen?"

"Seers are here only to maintain a balance between good and evil. Your inability to feel empathy towards your victims indicates you may have crossed the line. And you know once that line is crossed, you have inadvertently invited the Shadowman inside your heart. I sprayed the mist on your arm and it reacted positively. That thing left his mark on you. Little by little your soul will succumb to the evil that lurks within. After time, the light you have as a Seer will be extinguished by darkness."

"What?! What are you saying? You're telling me I have let the Shadowman inside?! You must be out of your fucking mind you spineless piece of shit!" And with those few words, I knew it was true.

"I'll go get your husband now," he replied, ignoring my last comment, standing to leave. "Wait here, I'll be right back."

Tears rolled down my face. What the hell had I done? My thirst for blood had inadvertently jeopardized my unborn child. I was infected with the Shadowman! Oh my God! I wanted to scream from the top of my voice and scratch this evil out of my soul. But it was already too late, no one ever got rid of a Shadowman without dying.

"Aria?" Elijah burst through the door. "Is it true?"

"Stop being a pussy and start acting like a man!" I shouted.

Elijah stopped short and looked at me like a man lost. He dropped down on his knees and hugged me close. "We're going to fight this thing. It will not win. God help us, I am not going to let this creature take my wife and child from me!"

"I'm sorry Elijah. I'm so sorry..." I cried.

"Doctor is there anything we can do? Something to stop the progression? Please, you've got to help us." Elijah pleaded.

Doctor Watts rubbed his baby face and replied, "I may know someone who can help you. Wait here, I'll be right back. Um, while I'm out, tell Aria what we spoke about."

"What is he talking about, baby? Tell me what?" I asked.

Elijah looked away, struggling to find a way to tell me.

"Please... Tell me, I have to know."

"Doctor Watts said eventually I won't be able to live in the same house as you. Once you start to show the physical traits of the Shadowman, I will be obligated to carry out my duties as a Seer. Otherwise, first I will turn and then the baby...."

"No, no, no! This cannot be happening!" I started to scream, feeling like I had lost my mind.

"Aria baby, please calm down! He said the progression can take months. It's not instantaneous so we still have time to search for a cure."

"We're going to be okay. I'm going to get through this. Everything is going to be alright," I repeated the mantra hoping it would take hold.

The doctor returned with an old Native American woman. In contrast to Doctor Watts, she was ancient. "Aria, Elijah, I'd like to introduce Sanjay. She is what we like to refer to as an *Elder Seer*."

CHAPTER THREE

I immediately moved into Sanjay's house, located on agency grounds. Her close proximity to the Agency made her accessible on a moment's notice. Everyone called her Grandmother because of her age, as well as her wisdom. Her three bedroom house was small and cozy with just enough room to not bump into each other. In the past, the Agency often requested her assistance in extreme cases involving junior Seers. In exchange, she lived a very comfortable life and never wanted for anything.

She placed me on a diet restricting all processed foods in an effort to rid my body of deadly toxins. I drank an herbal tea guaranteed to cleanse the bowels and the soul. I also mediated and prayed at least three times a day. When I wasn't praying, I read my Bible.

Sanjay exposed me to the mist on a daily basis, hoping to build up my resistance and drive the creature within away. Sometimes I would have a strong reaction, other times nothing at all. There was no way of knowing if it this was working or not. Not until it didn't.

Month after month went by. My baby continued to grow stronger by the day. Elijah came to visit when Sanjay said it was alright. Her strength as an Elder Seer made her resistant to a Shadowman's touch. Unfortunately, Elijah's powers weren't as strong. We all decided it was best to limit his exposure until we were certain I was no longer able to infect him.

I hated being without my husband. He was my rock, but he was also a very dedicated Seer. Neither of us wanted to be put in the situation of forcing him to meet his commitment to the cause.

Having made it to my eighth month of pregnancy, getting around became more difficult by the day. My back ached, my feet were swollen, and my temper was short. But I persevered and knew if I could make it to delivery; me and my baby would have a chance of making it out okay.

On one bright, beautiful sunny day, Sanjay was out in the garden picking fresh vegetables for lunch as she normally did. However, on this particular day, she needed assistance. "Aria? Aria, please come out to the garden. I need your help!" she called.

I heard her, but chose to ignore her calls for help. I was tired and my back hurt so badly the last thing I wanted to do was pick vegetables. I stayed inside and continued to watch television. I heard the back door slam.

"Aria? Aria?" she called out, coming into the

living room to find me sitting in front of the TV. "Girl, didn't you hear me calling you?! My foot got caught in the fence and I needed your help to get it unstuck."

I looked at the old woman with her papery thin skin, yellowed teeth, scraggly white hair, and hunched over back. She disgusted me with her constant bickering about do this, do that. I wanted her to leave me the hell alone. "If you say one more goddamned thing, I'm going to cut your fucking throat!" I yelled.

Sanjay stepped back in surprise. She knew this was not pregnancy hormones causing me to lose my temper, but suspected something more sinister. Her reaction was cool and measured because in her eighty plus years as a Seer, she had literally seen it all.

"Aria, come here please. I want to see your eyes." She requested in a kind grandmotherly voice.

"Go fuck yourself!" I replied, feeling not an ounce of respect for the woman who'd been my caretaker for the past six months. In that moment and for no good reason, I hated every fiber of her being.

Sanjay placed the basket of vegetables on the counter and walked over to the TV. She calmly picked up the remote and shut the television off. "Aria, I need to see your eyes. Now!"

The unaffected part of me finally reacted and got my butt off the couch. I walked over to the old woman, stooped down to her level, and opened my eyes wide so she could peer in.

"Oh dear Jesus! Your eyes have started to turn. The pupils are completely black and the whites have started to redden. This isn't working." Sanjay returned to the kitchen. "There's only one thing left to do."

I ran to the mirror and saw my own reflection staring back at me. For a brief moment, my eyes went entirely dark then returned back to normal. My heartbeat nearly jumped from my chest. I rubbed my swollen belly feeling my baby kick. I started to cry.

"Now, now dear. Don't fret. It's not over yet. There's still a chance for you and your baby. Listen to me carefully, everything we've done so far has only slowed down the progression, not stopped it fully. What I am going to suggest, I've only done one other time. I can't tell you how it ended out because I never heard from the man again."

"Sanjay, I'll do anything. Tell me what to do, please!" I begged.

"This goes against everything a Seer knows and believes. Tell no one what you're about to do. Not even Elijah. If you tell him, you will put him in extreme danger. Do you understand?'

"Sanjay, I promise I won't say anything to anyone. Please, go on."

"Hate to say it, but child, you've got to visit the original Shadowman—the devil himself."

I listened to the old woman speak about things I didn't want to hear.

"You've got to travel to the end of the world and meet him on his turf. Last chance you have is to ask for mercy." Sanjay anxiously wrung her hands. She knew what she had asked and the small chance of success.

"I don't think I can do that Sanjay. I've killed so many... What happens if I don't go?" I asked, weighing the possibilities and considering the consequences.

"In time the Shadowman will completely take over your soul. Maybe even your baby's. I'm sorry chile, I wish I had better news." Sanjay went into her bedroom and made the phone call.

I sank down into the worn sofa. The large number of kills I made and the innocent souls I set free, was all for naught. Because of one careless mistake, my soul and the soul of my unborn child were at stake. I had no choice.

"Tell me what I need to do."

CHAPTER FOUR

Under the guise of night, Sanjay and I strolled off the sacred agency grounds. "Sanjay, I want to thank you for helping me and my baby while I'm still able. You're risking your life to save mine. I don't know how I can ever repay you."

"Get out of his alive with your soul intact, that's how you can repay me," she whispered, almost out of breath.

We walked for about a mile and met up with two Native American men driving a pickup truck. They squeezed both of us between the two of them in the front seat. Neither said a single word, just drove.

A few hours later, the driver pulled off the main highway unto a dirt road and travelled for another hour. Under the overcast sky, the darkness of the night was absolute. My powers as a Seer were gone—nonexistent, for very little light remained inside me. I could actually feel the darkness taking over one cell at a time. The urge to pull the steering wheel to the side, causing the truck to crash was overwhelming. The only thing that stopped me was the thought of killing my unborn child.

The driver abruptly pulled off the road into

an open field bordered by a hilly outcropping on one side. The dim light of the full moon had come out and gently illuminated a small structure in the distance. I could barely make out a group of individuals milling around in the dark. Me and Sanjay got out of the truck and started walking towards the group. After we were out, the driver pulled off as quickly as he stopped.

"Sanjay," I whispered. "Where are we?"

She exhaled and shuddered despite the warmth of the night air. "We are at the mouth of hell. The people you see are *Supreme Seers*. All are full blooded Cherokee—*A ni yun wi yah*, which in English means 'The people of God'. Their powers are a thousand times more powerful than mine. The Agency reconnoiters these openings and assigns our most powerful masters to monitor the gates. They send these creatures back to hell before they can escape into our world."

The flimsy structure covered a gaping hole in the side of the hill. One Supreme Seer manned the openings at a time. The Agency determined ten minutes was the amount of time a Supreme Seer could withstand before any permanent damage was done to their supernatural abilities. The Supreme Seer's only purpose was to keep the dark evil spirits from escaping through the gates of hell. Once out in the world, they became

Shadowmen. Occasionally one slipped out undetected, but most times not.

The stench of sulfurous gas emanating from the opening caused my throat to constrict. I heard muffled screams which sounded like they came from within the hillside. The screams were inhuman, filled with sounds of agony and suffering. I wanted to turn and leave, but an unseen force took hold and drew me closer.

My feet moved in the direction of the structure against my will. My baby twisted and turned, kicking me strongly, as if he were doing everything to get my attention to make me turn back. It didn't work. I was in a daze and the only sounds I heard were deafening shrieks of terror. Yet I continued to gravitate towards the gate.

"Aria! Stop! Don't go any closer! This isn't what I planned! You can't go in there by yourself! Wait!" Sanjay shouted and tried to grab my arm.

I shrugged her off and continued towards the gaping hole in the side of the hill. When I was almost at the opening, I heard something calling out to me in a loving voice. Part of me was frightened; the other felt it was my destiny.

"Stop her! We can't let her go in! Please somebody stop her!" Sanjay pleaded.

Sanjay's old wrinkled hands grab at my arms. I looked at her with such hatred in my eyes and in my heart. With both hands and with all my might, I grabbed the old woman and shoved her towards the hole. Her mouth opened in shocked surprise at my actions. And just as quick, dark shadowy figures formed and pulled the old woman deep into their madness. I heard her screams of pain and fright. I smiled. I was pleased.

The remaining Supreme Seers tackled me to the ground. I awoke from my daze after realizing what I did to Sanjay. I cried out, "Sanjay! God, please help me! I don't want to die! Please protect my child." A handful of the old woman's hair remained tangled between my fingers. I looked at the gaping hole. Her screams became faint until I no longer heard them at all.

The commotion broke the trance of the Supreme Seer monitoring the gate. He looked in my direction and scowled, "Woman! Come to me!" he ordered.

I walked to where the Supreme Seer sat and I hung my head in shame. My soul was not completely tainted; some good still remained. Yet at the same time, I wanted to kill the Supreme Seers and throw them one by one into the gaping hole.

"Why are you here?" he asked.

"I was trying to kill a fully developed Shadowman. I let it touch me. The old woman,

Sanjay, brought me here to rid me of it. It grows stronger everyday and pretty soon I won't be able to fend it off. I'm frightened not only for myself, but also for my baby." I rubbed my stomach, feeling the reassuring kicks.

He touched my forehead and said, "The child you carry is unharmed. The Shadowman wants only your soul. I see your aura. You were once a Seer and have killed many. It wants revenge." He studied me as if he read my mind.

"Yes, I used to be a Seer. Now all I want is the blood of men, women, and children on my hands. I want to kill as many of you as I did of them. I want to hold your hearts in my bare hands until they stop beating and see the faces of my victims as they slip from life to death. I want to inhale their last breaths." I felt the darkness get closer to overtaking my soul and I embraced it. "The Shadowmen are no longer my enemy. I am the Shadowman!" I proudly exclaimed.

The Supreme Seer dropped his hand and backed away. "What kind of abomination are you? You were born a Seer; placed here on this earth to fight off evil. Yet now you have embraced it? What happened to you?!"

"When I was a Seer, I killed so many Shadowmen, death no longer bothered me. Perhaps you can say I lost my way trying to do the right thing. Ridding the world of Shadowmen no longer satisfied me. Killing became my drug. The more I killed, the more I wanted to kill, the more I had to kill. And I will continue killing until I am no longer able to." The voices calling out became louder and stronger. I covered my ears to quiet them.

"You are extremely close to being fully taken over, but I want you to fight. You need to fight for the sake of your baby! I think I know what Sanjay planned for you. Go outside and wait for me."

I pushed back the strong urge to dive headfirst into the hole, and obediently did as I was told. The Supreme Seer was replaced by another outside the gate. The old man held unto my arm, led me towards a small building, took me inside and pointed to a stool. I sat.

He opened a cabinet and retrieved an elaborately decorated decanter. From it, he poured a strong smelling orange liquid into a matching cup. "Drink this," he instructed.

"What is it? Will it harm my baby?" I asked, sniffing the liquid. It smelled of overly ripened oranges.

"No, but it will allow you to travel to the other side safely—in spirit form. Any other method is too dangerous. If you were to physically enter the gates of hell, your body and soul would be lost forever," he explained.

"If that's true, what happened to Sanjay's spirit? To her soul?" asked the decent part of me which still remained.

"Her physical body is no longer. However, because her spirit was strong and pure, those demons had no effect on Sanjay. She has already been lifted into the light. I felt her soul ascend into Heaven. She is safe."

"Thank God! I don't know what got over me."

"Yes, you do. Now drink."

I gulped down the orange liqueur tasking concoction. The warmth of the sweet drink coursed through my veins and into my heart. My heart beat slowed until it hardly beat at all. Barely able to keep my eyes open, I climbed onto a small cot I noticed in a dark corner of the room. The cot started to spin as if I were drunk. I developed tunnel vision which put me in a dense, dark airless space. The thought occurred— perhaps a bit too late, that I had been poisoned.

CHAPTER FIVE

"Aria, Seer of light, I command you to come to me." Called out a menacing voice in the darkest of places. My now poor eyesight was of no use in the impenetrable darkness. I had no idea where I was, but I was not frightened.

"Who are you? Why do you call my name as if you know me?" I asked feeling for something familiar—anything to hold on to. I thought I must be in a vacuum for there was no sound.

"Who am I? I am you," the voice replied.

"Why do you speak in riddles? Who are you?!"

"Aria, I am the darkness, the place mortal humans fear. I am everywhere and I am nowhere. I live inside men in the remote corners of their hearts; I am in the air you breathe and the food you eat."

"Why am I here? What is this place? Why can't I see?" I asked.

"Look inside yourself for the answers you seek. All you seek is within."

"I am here to ask mercy for my child. That is all I seek." The air shifted around me. A touch as gentle as the stroke of a feather brushed against my bare arm.

"Slayer of demons, you dare come to ask a

favor of me?" Something wet slithered over my foot. I jumped.

"Yes, please spare my baby from the touch of the Shadowmen. I know my soul is marked, but I beg of whoever you are, to please release my child from the hold you have on me." The sound of wings fluttering caused me to swat at the air. I heard and felt warm, putrid breath bearing down on my neck. Something hot touched my arm. I swatted it away. My hand connected with what could only be described as how I imagined a snake to feel.

"Your soul shall soon belong to me. Your baby belongs to you, thus your baby's soul shall also belong to me."

The voice was louder, clearer, stronger. Near. The sickeningly sweet smell of rotting flesh caused me to gag. "Tell me, what must I do to make this not so? I will do anything. Just tell me! Please!"

"Serve me! Bow down to me! Embrace the darkness! Accept your destiny! Give up your soul willingly and I will spare your child!"

A momentary flash of light in the distance provided a glimpse of the creature standing before me. The thing I saw was hideous and deformed. It resembled every horrible picture man had ever produced of how he imagined the devil would look. The demon oozed slime from its snakelike skin and grotesque rat like creatures scurried around its hooked feet. Its eyes were not eyes but images of lost souls twisting and turning in agony. The thing reached its deformed hand, dripping with squirming maggots, towards my face.

I started to scream hysterically. And continued screaming until the Supreme Seer slapped me back to my senses. I awoke drenched in sweat, with my heart beating powerfully in my chest.

"Wake up! You're fine! You're back with me. You're safe!" he cried shaking me back to reality.

I cried out, "It was horrible! Awful! I can't give my soul to that creature. Tell me what I have to do. Help me! Please!" I begged.

"You have seen the origin of the demons we call Shadowmen. He sends these spirits into our world to destroy everything good and pure. Shadowmen are everywhere. We Seers do our best to rid the world of them, but they outnumber us and seem to increase by the minute. They are everywhere!"

"But why? Why does it want me? Why does it want mine and my baby's souls?" I massaged my stomach trying to calm my baby down. A sharp pain registered in my back. I needed to relax.

"Because you are a Seer who lost her way. It thinks if it can get to you, he can get to all Seers. If that were to happen, all of humanity will be lost," explained the Supreme Seer.

"Then I've got to do something. Help me," I begged.

"I already have," he explained. "When I sent you to meet that thing, I hoped you still maintained some semblance of light—of goodness within. I took a chance and prayed a bit of Seer remained in your soul. It appears it does, otherwise you would never have been able to see within the eternal darkness."

"I don't understand. What do you mean?"

"It means there still may be a chance for you. The serum you drank has the potential to end the madness and also save your child, unless you're already too far gone." He stated.

"What do I do? Sanjay said my soul was almost completely taken over by the Shadowman. I don't have anywhere to go. My husband is also a Seer." Another sharp pain shot through my body.

"I'm sorry, but you will never be a Seer again, but possibly you may be able to control the Shadowman from growing any stronger. We must locate your husband. Your child is on its way."

I looked up at him in a panic, "What? How do you know?" The baby kicked again. I thought about Elijah. "Won't he be in danger with me?"

"Trust me. I know what I'm doing. We've got to get you out of here. This is no place to bring an innocent life into the world."

* * *

We took another pickup truck back to town. Morning was rapidly approaching and the sun was beginning to rise. The truck kicked up a trail of dust as the driver rushed to get me back to civilization before my baby came. It took several hours to make it to my house, but finally we did.

One look at my house and all the uncontrollable impulses to maim and destroy went away. I prayed I left any evil in my heart in that hellish place I visited. My labor pains were closer together. The driver helped me to the door, made sure someone was home, then returned to his truck for his journey back.

"Elijah! Baby, I'm home. Elijah, honey where are you?" I walked through the house to the bedroom.

"Aria? Is that you? What are you doing here? Where is Sanjay?" He walked towards me and hesitated.

"Baby, don't I get a hug?"

"Aria, please forgive me, but I have to ask? Are you okay? Sanjay said we shouldn't touch."

"I think its okay for you to touch me. Sanjay's gone... and I'm in labor. I need you to get me to the hospital. Right away," I explained and went to the bathroom to freshen up. The house looked the same. It needed a thorough cleaning, but all in all, Elijah was doing alright.

Although Elijah probably had hundreds of questions to ask, he took immediate action and retrieved the suitcase from we packed months earlier from the closet. He gently helped me in the car and drove like a bat out of hell....excuse the expression...straight to the hospital.

While Elijah filled out the paperwork, the nurse wheeled me into a private delivery room. The pains were closer and stronger. By the time I made it to the delivery room, they were so unbearable, I requested anesthesia to help ease the labor. The epidural made everything seem better. I relaxed, allowing the labor to progress. I closed my eyes and let the medicine take full effect.

"Push Aria! It's coming! Give me one more good push!" encouraged a nurse who reminded me of Nurse Jackie.

I bore down with all my might and pushed until I was about to burst. The next sound I heard was a baby crying. The nurse placed the baby to my breast.

I looked at my beautiful baby. With a head full of black curly hair, she was perfect in every way. Then she opened her eyes. They were pitch black! She smiled a treacherous smile, like the smile I witnessed on the face of that demon hours earlier. I started to scream and kept screaming uncontrollably for what felt like an eternity. The demons surrounded me laughing as if they'd won.

"Aria, wake up. Wake up dear, you just gave birth to a beautiful baby boy," said the nurse who looked like Aunt Esther from Sanford and Son.

I opened my eyes. I felt groggy, drugged, out of it. "What happened? Is everything okay? Where's my baby? Where's Elijah?" I asked. An uncomfortable mask covered my face, supplying me with oxygen, I suppose.

"You're fine dear and so is your son. We're required to keep you in the recovery room until we're certain you're okay. Your husband is in the waiting room."

"I had the baby? We have a son? How? I don't remember anything!" I explained, removing the mask.

"The baby was in a breeched position so the doctor performed an emergency caesarean. We had to put you under general anesthesia, but you have a perfect eight and a half pound baby boy!"

"When can I see him?" I asked, remembering the horrible dream. I needed to see his eyes.

"I'll get him right now. I was waiting for you to wake up," she replied. "Be right back."

I looked around the recovery room. An IV bag pushed fluids through a long clear tube attached to a needle penetrating my vein. It was taped to my wrist to keep it from moving. I wondered, *What would happen if I ripped the needle from my arm? Would an arc of blood squirt from the opening? Or would it slowly seep out until the blood coagulated at the site, forming a tacky scab over the wound.* I watched the slow drip, drip, drip while I waited for the nurse to return with my newborn child.

"Here he is Mrs. Griffin, your son." She wheeled in a cart containing a small clear bassinet, resembling a large shoe box. The infant squirmed as if he were trying free himself of the tightly wrapped blanket.

I looked at the baby, surprisingly feeling no emotion—no attachment whatsoever. I could've been looking at a toy doll. He seemed okay. "Can I hold it?" I needed to see its eyes.

"No, not yet, you're not strong enough. We'll bring him back in a couple of hours so you can feed him. By then you should be able to sit up," replied the nurse.

"It's asleep. Can you shake him? You know, wake it up? I need to see its eyes." I insisted.

"He's fine, he'll wake up soon. Don't worry, your baby is fine." The nurse smiled down at my little bundle of joy.

"Wake him up goddamnit!" I yelled.

"Mrs. Griffin! There's no need for that kind of language!" she replied with a shocked expression.

"Go screw yourself, you old Aunt Esther looking bitch!" I added.

She stormed from the room, taking the baby with her. "Well I never!" she exclaimed.

I never saw his eyes, but I already had my answer. He was fine, I wasn't. I pulled myself up to sit. After gathering my bearings, I noticed a metal tray covered by surgical instruments. I carefully slid the objects to the side and picked up the tray. When I observed my reflection—saw my eyes, I dropped the tray on the floor and screamed.

"Mrs. Griffin? Are you alright?" asked a different nurse.

I fought back the Shadowman's strong urge to overtake me and said, "Nurse, please get my husband, Elijah. Tell him it's urgent."

"Actually I was on my way to return you to your room. Can it wait for about ten minutes?" asked the nurse.

I said a silent prayer and was able to suppress the evil spirit—for the time being. I watched as the nurse unhooked me from several machines and prepped me for relocation. She and an orderly wheeled me down the hall, past the nursery and into my room. Elijah stood at the door watching it all. I looked at him and instinctively understood. He knew. He turned away and sighed deeply.

"Aria, our son is fine. He's not infected," he replied still standing in the doorway, unwilling and unable to come any closer.

"Take the baby home Elijah. Love him with all your heart. When you tell him stories about his mother, let him know I was once a really good Seer—before embracing the darkness into my soul."

"I understand," he whispered. "You realize I can't *be* a Seer right now? I can't destroy the woman I love, no matter what evil lurks within you." He fought his own personal demon, the instinct of a Seer to kill me—the Shadowman.

The Shadowman's power grew stronger yet amazingly, I was able to control it. I felt it try to take over my soul and harden my heart towards Elijah, but I fought it. Now I finally understood what the Supreme Seer did for me. He had allowed my baby to remain safe by delaying the progression of the Shadowman's development. With a glimpse inside the horrific bowels of hell, I conjured up the remaining goodness I held as a Seer and used it to fight against the evil forces inside me. I could keep it in check. The Supreme Seer was right, I was an abomination.

"I'm sorry Elijah. I never meant for any of this to happen. As much as I want to come home with you and the baby, I can't. It's not safe for any of us. Please take our son home and forget about me. I'm no good for either of you."

"Aria, I love you." His eyes filled with tears. "I don't think I can do this without you. Maybe we can get help. Find someone who can rid you of this thing."

Looking at Elijah, I realized there was only one way to make him understand we could never be a family. Although I could control this thing, I would never be totally rid of what resided inside. I summoned all the love I felt and replied, "I don't love you. I will never love you. You make me sick!"

"I know what you're doing Aria and it's not going to work." He stepped towards me.

"Stop! Don't come any closer. Don't you know who I am?" I asked.

"Yes, you're Aria, my wife and the mother of my child."

"No, you're wrong. I am the Shadowman." I

released the evil for just a moment to let Elijah see what I truly was. I felt the coldness seep into every cell of my body. And as quickly as I let the Shadowman out, I quickly put it back down.

My husband stopped dead in his tracks and looked at the woman he once loved—still loved. He reached deep into his pocket and withdrew a necklace. "Here, take this with you. I've been carrying it around since I found out you were pregnant. It's a locket with a picture of us inside. I added Elijah Jr.'s picture just a few moments ago." He tossed the necklace to me, dropped his head and walked away in surrender. Elijah never looked back.

A couple of days later, I was well enough to leave the hospital. I packed up my things, hitchhiked across the country, and ended up in a little town outside of Fairbanks, Alaska. I figure most of the year it's too cold to come outside, so the exposure to people is greatly reduced. I fingered the necklace, pressing the locket to my lips and kissed the image of my husband and son. So far, I haven't killed anyone. But, there's always tomorrow…

THE END

GREATVIEW ISLAND

CHAPTER ONE

"Alphonse, it's perfect! I can't wait for you to see the house!" Monique exclaimed.

"Where did you say it is again? It sounded like you said Greatview Island!" he laughed.

"That *is* what I said. The realtor said the house has been on the market for a while and we can get it for way under market value. I viewed it earlier today and I absolutely love it!"

"Greatview Island, huh? Ain't that where all the rich folks of Harperstown live? And you're telling me one of those houses is being sold for under market value? What's wrong with it?" he asked skeptically.

"Nothing! It's a two level traditional beach house with four bedrooms, three full baths, updated appliances, and hardwood floors throughout. And it's only a block from the beach!"

"Alright, it sounds pretty good. I'd like to check it out. Can Rachel meet us after work today? Say around five?"

"Hold the line, I'll give her a call and find out." Monique clicked the other line and dialed Rachel.

"Rachel's Realty, we only serve the best," she answered.

"Hey Rachel, it's me Monique. I have Alphonse on the other line. He wants to see the house at five. Are you available to show it then?"

"Sure Monique, Five o'clock sounds perfect. I'll just be finishing up an open house and will meet you guys there."

"Thanks, Rachel." She clicked back to Alphonse. "Hey baby, she says she can meet us there. I'm so excited because I know you're going to love it too."

"Anything to keep my woman happy. I'll pick you and AJ up around four thirty. We'll all ride over together."

"Alphonse, after all this time looking, I think we've finally found our home. I'm so happy! I can't wait for you to see it."

"Monique, take a deep breath and calm down. I'll see you in a few hours, okay?" he chuckled at his wife's overly excited reaction.

"You're right. I'm not going to get crazy until you've had a chance to see the place. After all, you've got to love it as much as I do. I'll see you soon. I love you."

"Love you too, baby."

Alphonse knew of Greatview Island, but neither he nor any of his friend's had ever visited the secluded, exclusive enclave of affluent neighborhoods. Growing up in the *unofficially* segregated city of Harperstown, blacks lived on one side of the city while whites lived on the other. Greatview Island was on the *other* side. Because of the unwritten rule of segregation, the island had always been off limits as far as he was concerned.

"You've lived here all your life—almost thirty years, and have never been to Greatview Island? How is that even possible?" Monique asked.

"Baby, you were raised as an Air Force brat and have lived all over the world, so you don't understand how people naturally segregate themselves. Although whites and blacks went to the same schools, we lived in different neighborhoods. They stuck to their own kind and we stuck to ours. That's just the way it was, and still is as far as I'm concerned." Alphonse pointed to a flag flying off a rickety old house. "Look. See that's what I mean."

Monique looked in the direction of his ire. An old civil war, confederate flag hung proudly from a flagpole extending from a shotgun style house. She noticed several other houses also flying the confederate flag.

"Daammnnn! I haven't seen this many confederate flags since I visited South Carolina a few years back. It's kinda strange to see how blatantly people display them!" she exclaimed.

"Well, I'm from Virginia and I see this all the time, so I would really prefer not to have my child see these racist symbols every time we come home." He looked in the back seat at his son. "Sure do hope there's another street leading to this friggin' neighborhood."

"Honey, it's not that bad and times have changed to where we *can* live wherever we choose. Anyway pretty soon, we won't even notice those flags. Trust me, this house is worth having to drive a couple of miles through 'hicksville'," she snickered.

Alphonse followed the long winding road for several miles passing through the small town that looked as if it were a throwback to the 1950's. The main street consisted of a general store, a small post office, and several mom and pop shops selling antiques—mostly civil war memorabilia. *The town that time forgot. And apparently so did the civil rights movement!*

As they reached the outskirts of the town, the land changed to resemble more of a boggy marsh. Turning the last corner, they came upon a covered bridge that appeared to have been there since the original inhabitants took up residence. A stream of water barely a foot deep trickled underneath the structure. *"Welcome to Greatview*

Island! From sunrise to sunset, every day is a vacation. Population—it depends" was painted above the entrance.

"Almost there," Monique said excitedly. "After we cross the bridge, make a right on Lakeview. The house is all the way at the end— on the left."

"Well, I'll be... I never knew all this was back here. Hmmm, not bad—not bad at all."

The neighborhood on the right consisted of newly constructed, customized, and very expensive looking single family homes. Most were finished in white siding; however several were painted in vibrant tropical colors reminiscent of beach towns in Florida. On the other side of the road, the residents seemed to prefer the weather worn style of beach homes to the expensive ones recently built. In spite of the obvious differences, both styles of homes seemed to fit.

"There's the house! What do you think? Isn't it beautiful?" Monique gushed. "Look, you can see the beach from here!" She jumped from the car before Alphonse had a chance to park.

"Hey, calm down woman! Next time give me a chance to stop before you open the door!" He shook his head at his wife's eagerness.

"Daddy, I wanna see too!" exclaimed AJ.

Rachel was already at the home. She stood on

the front porch and hoped this family would be the last she'd have to show the house to. In her twenty odd years as a realtor, this house proved to be the most difficult to sell. So far, the house had been listed for over a year, and that was after the owners took it off the market for a couple of months. Since the last family moved, the property stood vacant for almost three years. It seemed once potential buyers heard about the history of the house, their interest quickly evaporated. As required by law, Rachel told Monique the history of the home to explain why the price was so low. Monique didn't seem to care, and hopefully she would convince her husband to think the same way.

"Hey guys, how you doing?" asked Rachel. She thought *they seem like such a nice family. I really hope the stories about this house aren't true. Sure wouldn't want to see them get hurt.*

"Hi Rachel, this is my husband Alphonse and our son."

"Alphonse, nice to meet you. And who do we have here?" she asked, stooping down to AJ's level.

"My name is Alphonse Junior, but everybody calls me AJ." He lifted his shirt and started to chew the fabric—a nervous tic he developed recently while talking to strangers.

"Well, I am so pleased to meet you AJ. How old are you?"

He held up four fingers and stated, "I'm four and I'm going to have a huge party on my fifth birthday. You can come if you want to."

"Thanks for inviting me, I'll try to make it," Rachel replied. "Hey AJ, do you like the beach?"

"Yessss..."

"Maybe your Mommy and Daddy can walk you down there later. Would you like that?"

He nodded his head and jumped up and down excitedly. "Daddy, can we go to the beach? Please, can we?"

"Yes son, but first Mommy and Daddy need to look at the house. You stay close to us and don't go wandering away. You understand?" Alphonse knew how anxious his son would be to get to the water, but he didn't want that to distract him from touring the house. From the outside, he had to admit, it looked fabulous.

"Yes sir, I understand." He reached for Monique's hand and held on tightly. "I promise I'll be a good boy."

Rachel gave the couple a tour of the 3000 square foot home from top to bottom, including the lovely master suite upstairs, a huge bonus room which also served as a game room, two spacious living spaces and a kitchen that would impress any accomplished chef. Alphonse took one look at the wood burning fireplace in the living room and was almost sold; that is until Rachel showed them the showpiece.

"And now for the best part of the house, I'll take you outside to the deck." Rachel opened the French doors to a covered deck that spanned the width of the house.

"Wow!" Alphonse took in the beautiful scenery. The island had been previously designated as a natural preserve by the city of Harperstown, which meant no further development would take place at the back of the property. As far as he could see, the boggy marsh stretched on for miles. Birds of all species flocked to the area, flying in perfect formation as if they were dancing.

"Honey, what do you think?" Monique asked, pleased with finding such a gem.

"I love it! It's so peaceful and relaxing back here and I can see myself coming home from work and stretching out on this deck with a cold beer. Cool! The backyard is already fenced in, so it's safe for AJ to be out here while you're in the kitchen cooking. Honestly, I don't see a thing wrong with this house, which makes me wonder again; why is this house so inexpensive?"

Rachel looked at Monique inquisitively. From her expression, it was obvious she hadn't told her husband much about the house's history. She started to speak, but Monique interrupted her before she had a chance to answer Alphonse's question.

"Um, Rachel, can you give us a moment please? How about you show AJ the bedrooms upstairs again?" she asked.

"Oh, alright. Just give a yell when you're done. C'mon AJ, let's go look upstairs again." She reached for his hand and took him inside. She gave a backwards glance at Monique wondering if she should step in and tell Alphonse the whole truth.

Alphonse observed the nonverbal communication from the two women speaking in code. He knew his wife very well, so he stood back and waited for an explanation.

"Okay Monique, what's gives? What's the story behind this house? Why all the mystery? Did someone die here or something?" he laughed, but stopped laughing when he noticed Monique did not join in.

"Uh, well, yeah, that's sorta what happened. Come here, sit down."

They took a seat on the patio furniture left by the previous owners. The sun was just beginning to set over the marsh in a beautiful sunset and the sky took on unimaginable colors of beauty.

Alphonse didn't speak. He waited for his wife to share the history of the house.

CHAPTER TWO

"Rachel said the reason this house is being sold for fifty percent below value is because someone did die here."

"What?! How?" asked Alphonse, confused as to why a death could drastically reduce the price of the house.

"Well, they didn't *just* die. The guy who built this house came from a family of very wealthy land developers. It was only supposed to be their summer home, but he wanted it to be extra special for his wife and child. They were young, black professionals—kind of like us. Anyway, they'd only been married for a couple of years when they moved in. Shortly after moving in, the wife and two year old child went missing. The police said the boy probably climbed the fence and wandered into the marsh; he most likely got lost and the mother went in looking for him. They probably drowned or something because the land is soft like quick sand in some places. Their bodies were never recovered. The police report indicated the husband was so distraught over his family that he committed suicide a few months later. He hung himself in the game room. Supposedly, this house is haunted by his ghost because he's still looking for his family."

Alphonse sat back in the chair and exhaled. "No wonder they can't get rid of this house! So what do you think about this story? Doesn't this make you…concerned?"

"Tell you the truth, at first it did. But once I got to walking around here and *feeling* the house, it didn't bother me anymore. I actually feel very comfortable. You know I am not the slightest bit superstitious."

"That is quite a story. I don't know Monique... The man actually killed himself here. In this house." He looked around the huge deck and took in the spectacular view once again. "Yet still, it's an amazing house at a steal of a price."

"Baby, I'm not asking you to make an offer now. Let's just think it over. Okay?"

"Alright, that's fair. Let's sleep on it before making a decision."

Monique knew as soon as Alphonse agreed to think it over, she'd have her way and the house would soon be theirs.

She yelled out for Rachel and AJ, "Hey guys, come back downstairs. Let's go to the beach before it gets too dark!"

"Yay! We're going to the beach!" AJ yelled out in excitement as he ran down the stairs.

"Everything okay here? Did you tell Alphonse about the house—about its history?" she asked, looking between the two.

Monique nodded her head. Alphonse simply shrugged and exhaled loudly. Rachel watched the couple's reaction. She knew without a doubt Monique was in. Alphonse on the other hand was still on the fence.

"Alphonse, if you have any questions, please ask. I don't want to sell you this house unless you're absolutely one hundred percent certain you want it. It is a beautiful house at a great price, but that doesn't mean anything if you aren't comfortable living in it." Rachel added. She'd witnessed too many buyers experience buyer's remorse after realizing they were in over their heads. As a professional, she prided herself on not only selling houses to her clients, but finding them actual homes.

"Thanks Rachel. We're going to sleep on it and make a decision soon. But for now, we're going to take our son to the beach before he bursts!" added Alphonse, watching his son jump up and down.

"Alright, well, I'll go ahead and lock up." She walked the family to the door. "Oh, since tomorrow's Saturday, why don't you guys come out and take a look. Get a feel for the neighborhood."

"That's a great idea. We'll be in touch." Monique waved goodbye and followed her husband and son to the beach.

* * *

"If you're sure, then I'm willing to go for it," replied Alphonse to his wife as she prepared his breakfast.

"I'm sure. And with the money we'll save on the house, I can quit my job and stay home with AJ until he starts school. That house is perfect for us. It's almost as if it were built just for me. I don't want to change a thing." She sipped from a steaming mug of coffee.

"And the suicide ghost thing doesn't bother you?"

"We'll ask the bishop to come bless the house before we move in."

"Alright, if it will keep my woman happy, then we'll call Rachel first thing Monday morning and tell her to put in our offer."

"Thank you, thank you, thank you! Baby, I promise we won't regret this decision." Monique was happy they'd decided to visit the neighborhood both days. The beach on Saturday was very busy. Both locals and tourists alike strolled through the streets, casually dressed in bathing suits and flip flops. Sunday was different; as the beach was filled mostly with locals zipping around on golf carts or out walking the ever present family dog.

CHAPTER THREE

The movers delivered their furniture during the first week of June. Monique quit her job and Alphonse took time off from his to get moved in as quickly as possible. Coming from a cozy apartment, they didn't have much furniture to fill such a large house. Both were busily unpacking when they heard the front door open.

"Hello?" Called out a woman's voice from the front door.

"Who in the world is that? I didn't hear the doorbell. You expecting company?" asked Alphonse from the living room. He was in the middle of hanging artwork.

"No, but it sounds like she's already inside the house," responded Monique. She closed the kitchen cabinet where she was in the process of laying fresh cabinet liners and went to check on their uninvited guest.

"Hello, I hope you don't mind me letting myself in, but the door was ajar," replied the older white woman. She was tastefully dressed in tailored Bermuda shorts and a short sleeve expensive looking silk blouse. A thin strand of pearls enveloped her neck. Her bluish white hair was teased to perfection and held firm by a can of hair spray.

Monique responded in amazement at the woman's brazenness of entering her home without being invited. "Um, excuse me is there something we can do for you?" She wiped the sweat from her brow with a dishtowel.

"I saw cars parked outside. My husband and I just got back into town and I stopped by to welcome the new owners to the neighborhood. Are they here?" asked the woman, looking past Monique.

Monique whipped her head around and looked at Alphonse who appeared to have an '*I told you so*' look on his face. She approached the woman and said, "We're the owners. I'm Monique and this is my husband Alphonse."

"Oh? I didn't realize... *Oh my God!* She thought, *they're Negroes!* I'm so sorry for bothering you. Uh, excuse me I'll leave you to your work then." She turned to leave.

"I'm sorry. We didn't catch your name..." Monique watched the old woman squirm uncomfortably.

She quickly recovered her manners, cleared her throat and replied, "I'm Mrs. Stallworth. We bought our property a few years ago and you're only the second family to move in since we've lived here. The other couple who used to own the house was so nice. It was a shame they had to leave because they were a wonderful addition to the neighborhood. We used to have them over for coffee often."

"Thanks for stopping by Mrs. Stallworth. We're kind of busy right now, but maybe we can get together and have drinks later on." Monique added just to get a response from the busybody.

"Oh, well, that will be fine. Uh, except we don't drink. Um, I should go now. You two take care and remember this is a nice respectable neighborhood." She hightailed down the stairs and across the street.

"There goes the neighborhood!" Alphonse joked. "Told you there was a reason we never visited these parts growing up. Watch how quickly the news will spread about us—the new owners."

"Whatever. I don't care because in time they'll have to get used to us. Guess the other couple she talked about was a young respectable *white* couple. Humph, welcome to the neighborhood, indeed!" she laughed.

They returned to the chore of moving in. It was well past noon when they realized how hungry they were. The only food they had was in cans or boxes.

"Alphonse, what time did you say your mother was dropping off AJ?"

"She said around one. Why?"

"Honey, please ask her to pick up a pizza and something to drink on the way back. I'm starved and it takes too long to go out and get something to bring back."

"So now you realize how far from civilization we are? They probably don't even deliver pizza out this way. Gotta drive to Timbuktu and back just to get here. You better be glad I love you, woman," he joked.

"Man, will you please call your mother before she leaves?"

Alphonse phoned in his order and called his mother to have her pick up the pizza on the way to dropping off AJ.

* * *

"Hellooo, is anybody home?" Called out Alphonse's mother.

"Yeah Mom, we're in the kitchen. C'mon in. We're kind of tied up at the moment."

"Hey Monique. Hi son. I'm gonna put the pizza right here on the counter. Your father sent a six pack of beer, too. Said to tell you it's his house warming gift," she laughed.

"Hello Mother," replied Monique.

"Hi Mommy! Hi Daddy!" AJ ran up to give both his parents a hug.

"Hold on son! Mommy and Daddy are trying to hang this picture. Give us a minute. Okay?"

"Umh, umh, umh! This sure is a beautiful house! Do you mind if I look around?"

"No Mom, go right ahead. I'll be with you as soon as we get this picture up," replied Alphonse.

"Mommy, can I go outside?" asked AJ.

"Yes, but you stay on the deck."

All of a sudden, they heard Alphonse's mother scream. Both quickly lowered the heavy picture to the floor. Alphonse ran up the stairs with Monique at his feet. His mother stood in the game room holding her chest, covered in perspiration. She stared at the wooden beams that transversed the ceiling.

"Mom, what's the matter? Are you alright?!" He went to his mother.

Monique ran to the linen closet and pulled out a washcloth. She wet it with cool water, ran back in the game room and dabbed the cool cloth on her mother-in-law's face.

"I'm okay. I thought I saw something. Whew! That was strange!" She sank down to the floor and caught her breath.

"What happened? What did you see?" asked Monique, looking at the beams.

She looked at her son and his wife. They were so happy about the house she didn't want to ruin it by putting an old woman's fears in front of them. "Nothing dear, I must have been out in the heat too long chasing after AJ . I'm fine. Let's go back downstairs."

"Alright, if you're sure you're okay." Alphonse took the cloth from his wife.

"I'm fine. Where is AJ by the way?" she asked looking at Monique.

Realizing she had left her son on the back deck, she quickly returned downstairs to check on him. She ran to the back window and saw a strange sight. AJ stood at the fence staring off into the marsh, chewing nervously on his shirt. It appeared he was deep in conversation. From the vantage point of the kitchen window, she didn't realize how high the marsh grass was. It must've grown to at least six feet. Standing that close, her son looked tiny and helpless.

She went out to the deck and called out, "AJ? AJ, didn't I tell you to stay on the deck?! Get up here boy! Now!"

He turned to face his mother and answered, "Okay Mommy, I'm coming."

Monique watched in horror as her son waved to something in the grass. As he turned to run towards her, his little feet got tangled up and he tripped. The tall grass beyond the fence moved as if something were there. AJ turned from where he laid and also looked.

What the hell is out there? She ran out the French doors and bounded down the steps to where her son lay. She scooped him up in her arms and looked towards the marsh. The grass stirred again. She was about to turn and run when a flock of geese took flight from the spot where she focused. *I have got to get a hold of myself! Getting spooked over birds!*

"Didn't I tell you to stay on the deck?! There are all kinds of animals in the marsh. Until we know exactly what's out there, I don't want you going in the yard without me. Understand?!

"Sorry Mommy, but I heard somebody calling my name. They said, 'AJ, AJ, come here AJ'," he whispered in his little boy voice.

"Baby, there are no people in the marsh. Only animals live out there."

"Uh uh, Mommy, there *are* people who live there. They called my name," he insisted.

She dismissed her son's make believe story when she heard a strange clucking noise. "Do you hear that? Sounds like chickens."

"Look Mommy, they have chickens in their yard. Can I go over and pet them?" he asked, already distracted from the conversation about the marsh.

"What in the world?! You're right! Those are chickens! And there's a chicken coop, too!" She looked in her other neighbor's yard. They also had a chicken coop full of hens and roosters.

Alphonse and his mother came outside and stood on the deck. And just as everyone who had previously gazed upon the nature preserve, she was enthralled by the natural beauty.

"Is he okay?" asked Alphonse, coming down into the yard.

"Yeah, he's alright. He said someone called his name so he went to the marsh to check it out."

"What?! AJ, don't go making up stories! If you wanted to play in the backyard, you should've waited for me or Mommy to come out here with you. Come here big boy. You're too big to have your mother carry you around."

AJ pretended to show his muscles. "That's right, Daddy! I'm a muscle man."

"Yeah? You gonna protect Mommy when I'm not here, right?"

"Um hum, cause I am the man!" he exclaimed and high-fived his father.

"Go on inside so mommy and daddy can talk. Ask grandma to give you a slice of pizza." He swatted his son playfully on the rear.

They watched their son run inside to his grandmother. He was such an energetic child who never seemed to get tired.

"Is your mother alright?"

"Yeah, she said she was probably in the sun too long. They went to the playground before she brought AJ home. She's okay now. So, what happened out here?"

"I don't know," she shrugged. "When I came downstairs, AJ was standing at the fence. It looked like he was talking to someone. When I called for him to come inside he turned around and waved good-bye."

Simultaneously they realized how difficult it would be keeping him away from the fence—away from the marsh. And considering the story the realtor told them about the previous owners, *not* keeping him away was not an option.

"Hmm, that is strange. You think he made up an imaginary friend?"

"Don't think so, but it's nothing to worry about. I think it was just geese in the grass. Anyway, that's enough excitement for today. Let's eat, I'm starved."

Alphonse's mother left the island worried and afraid for her children. She didn't want to mention what she'd seen to either of the kids. It was too horrible to put to words.

The young black man's body hung limply from a rope thrown across one of the heavy wooden beams. His short afro was matted with dirt and his face was covered with stubble. The man appeared to be around thirty, but she couldn't really tell because he was so bloated. His bloodshot eyes bulged from their sockets as if they were about to pop out and fall to the floor. She saw the man's swollen tongue protrude from his mouth in a grotesque grin of death with bloody vomit dripping down the front of his shirt. The sight of his lifeless body was bad enough, but what really frightened her was when he turned his head and looked at her.

She anxiously wondered aloud, "What the heck happened in that house? I've got to tell Franklin so we can get to the bottom of this. That wasn't just an apparition I saw. Something much more sinister resides in those walls." She involuntarily shuddered.

CHAPTER FOUR

Over the next couple of weeks, Monique and Alphonse took long walks in the neighborhood to meet the neighbors. The young couple soon discovered the majority of the people who lived on their side of the island were from somewhere else entirely and only vacationed during the short summer season. Their attempts to be friendly were met with indifference. So one day while out trying to find more hospitable neighbors they made their way to the other side of the island and happened upon an outdoors neighborhood watch meeting.

"Will you please stand and introduce yourselves?" asked the neighborhood watch leader.

"My name is Alphonse and this is my lovely wife, Monique. We've just recently moved into the house on Lakeview Drive."

A collective sound of surprise reverberated throughout the small crowd. Many started whispering to one another, while others simply remained quiet shaking their heads.

"You mean the old Redman place?" asked an old man, standing apart from the others.

"I don't know about that, but the house we moved into has been vacant for quite a while," replied Alphonse.

"Damned shame what happened to those folks. I knew the girl's family very well," he said.

"Now, now, people, let's not get off track here. You can talk amongst yourselves later, but for now we're here to discuss any problems you are may be having with crime," the leader stated.

The group continued to discuss criminal activity or the lack thereof. Very few outsiders ventured on the island after dark because of the heavy police presence. It always seemed that the places with the lowest crime always had the most police. Without crime statistics to labor over, the group ended up planning the end of season block party.

"Thank you all for coming. And at the next neighborhood watch meeting, we will be bringing in a gang unit to talk about how to avoid the pressure of joining. For those of you with teenagers, please plan on bringing them along."

The group dispersed and headed towards their respective sections of the island. The temporary residents piled into their golf cars and headed across the road to the sanctity of their exclusive suburban enclave, while the other residents from the older section remained behind and mingled. Alphonse and Monique chose to stick around.

"Excuse me ma'am, I hope I didn't upset you

earlier with my reference to the Redman's," the old man said.

"No, not at all. I'd be interested in hearing more about the family, if you don't mind."

"First let me tell you something about that neighborhood you're in. Them uppity, rich folks don't want nothing to do with us long time residents, and probably not even you. They come down here and buy up them fancy houses and only stick around for the summer. Rest of the year, they gone and we're left to watch over their homes to keep thieves away. That's why this neighborhood watch is so important. We've got to look out for one another. By the way, name's Gus."

"Pleased to meet you Gus, I'm Alphonse and this is Monique. Thanks for the heads up about our neighbors, but I think we've already discovered we're not one of them. We ran into Mrs. Stallworth the first day we moved in. Funny we haven't seen her since. Have we honey?"

Monique shook her head while keeping an eye on AJ playing with another little boy.

"I know who she is and I wouldn't worry about seeing her after Labor Day. They usually pack up and leave until next season. I believe they're from upstate New York, New England, New Jersey or somewhere along the northeast coast. Most people who live on that side don't want to associate with a young black couple, such as yourselves—unless of course you're rich like the Redman's were. Anyway, I was going to tell you about that poor girl and her baby."

Everyone's ears within range perked up to listen. The man propped himself up against a tree and began speaking.

"Who were they?" asked Monique. "The realtor said he was a land developer."

"Yep, the Redman family was pretty big back in their day. That boy's family bought up most of the available land in Harperstown, which was unheard of for a black family back then. They owned most of the land over there on that side and started building up them houses about ten years ago. I bet them rich white folks didn't know nothing about the Redman's when they bought them houses."

"So what does that have to do with the woman who went missing?"

"Let me tell you. That land used to be a slave burial ground. This part of Virginia was heavily involved in the slave trade back in the 1700's. Them slave ships would get just close enough to land to throw them bodies overboard before they docked in the port a few miles south of here. Native Americans who used to live on these parts saw what was going on and decided to give the slaves a decent burial." The old woman paused to spit a wad of chewing tobacco on the ground.

She continued, "So for hundreds of years, they pulled bodies out of the ocean and buried them on that land. When the slave trade was finally over, they somehow rerouted the water so it would flood and become marshland. That swamp out there is where most of the bodies were buried. Your house and the houses that surround the marsh were built on top of that graveyard. Virginia designated most of this island as a nature preserve instead of calling it what it really was—a consecrated cemetery. Wasn't supposed to be no houses built over there—ever."

"If what you say is accurate, then how did the Redman's build on the land?" asked Alphonse.

"I can tell you how," added an elderly white woman, who was missing her front teeth. "It's because they found a loophole in the law. Somehow the state didn't properly designate all the land as being a nature preserve and them Redman's jumped right in and took advantage of that loophole. They considered this land prime real estate and saw no reason not to build. Serves them right for building over all those graves."

"Uh huh, that's right. Them slaves rose up and took that man's family. They sent something straight from the marsh to lure that boy in there.

It's supposed to be some kind of beast that comes out every now and then to feed. Summer ain't so bad because of the heat, but once fall and definitely winter comes, that thing is said to come out every night in search of food. Why you think them rich folks pack up and leave every year?"

Alphonse started to laugh, "Come on, you can't be serious! That's the most ridiculous thing I've ever heard. A monster from the marsh?! Seriously?!" he scoffed.

"Man, I am telling you the truth. That's why all the houses that back up to the marsh all got chickens in their backyards. They hope those chickens will satisfy the creature's appetite and it will leave them alone. The only reason they haven't sold their houses is they paid too much for them and can't find buyers. And if you ask any of them about it, they'll deny it. They don't want their real estate value to drop," Gus explained.

"So you're saying a monster from the marsh took Redman's wife and child?" asked Monique. She remembered AJ standing at the fence as if he were talking to someone. A cold chill traveled up her spine.

The old woman added, "Yep, we had a real bad nor'easter storm that year and the island was cut off from the rest of Harperstown. It must've rained for at least 48 hours straight and the road flooded. His family was one of the first to move in so weren't no neighbors around. Redman told the police he was upstairs and his wife and baby were in the kitchen. They were concerned about the house flooding because all day long they watched water from that marsh slowly creep into their yard. He said he went downstairs to check on 'em when he found the backdoor standing wide open. There was no sign of either of 'em. That boy searched the house like a madman and eventually ended up going into that water. Nobody has seen 'em since. The Redman boy didn't know the history when he built his house there, but his Papa knew and let him do it anyway. Come to find out that creature lured them into that marsh."

"The family finally told their son about the history of the land and his precious home when they couldn't find his wife and baby. They knew what happened. They never found the bodies but a couple of weeks later, a fisherman pulled that baby's coveralls out of that marsh on his fish hook. That boy couldn't take it no more and hung himself," Gus explained. He surprisingly became emotional and wiped a tear from his eye.

"Rachel didn't tell us that part of the story. She just said the husband was distraught and committed suicide because of the pain of losing his family."

"Umh, that's all she told you huh? Well, she must've gotten a big commission out of it anyways." Gus studied Monique closely. He squinted tightly and said, "You know you could pass for that girl's sister? Y'all kinda of resemble each other."

"Okay, that's enough ghost stories for today. We've got to get home before the monster comes out for its meal," joked Alphonse. He saw the look on Monique's face and became concerned she was falling for the old man's superstitious tales. "Monique, girl you don't believe all this bull crap do you? You're not superstitious, remember?"

The spell was broken. Monique shook off the *heebie jeebies* the old man and woman managed to give her. "Yeah baby, you're right. I don't believe in all this foolishness. Sounds like a bunch of old wives tales to me. You guys are just trying to scare me and I almost fell for it. C'mon AJ, let's go home. Nice meeting you Gus."

The old woman shouted out, "I'd advise you to get a few chickens or a small pet you're not very fond of to leave in the back yard. And whatever you do, don't go outside during a nor'easter!"

Gus and the old woman watched the family walk away. He prayed for their safety but knew better. The other family who used to live there had the same reaction before they fled from the house, leaving everything they owned behind.

When they arrived back at their house, the front door stood wide open and all the lights were turned on. The television blared loudly from the living room.

"What the hell is going on?! Monique, you and AJ go next door and call the police. I'm going to see if anyone's inside."

"Alphonse, don't go in the house! What if someone's still inside?! Baby, please stay with us and wait for the police to come. I've got my cell phone. I'll call right now."

"Oh, alright! It's probably some kids from the neighborhood pulling a prank. Go ahead and call."

Within minutes, two police cars arrived at the house with sirens blaring. The commotion caught the attention of the neighbors across the street. The Stallworths peeked out the window and shook their heads in disgust at how the new neighbors dared to disturb their peace. And the husband nonchalantly sipped from his martini as if watching a movie.

"Sir, what seems to be the problem?" asked one of the younger cops.

"We went for a walk and when we returned, this is what we found. Front door open, lights on, and television on full blast. I told my wife it was probably just a bunch of kids," Alphonse explained, looking around to see if any of the neighbors would come offer any assistance.

"You're new to the island, right?" he surveyed the couple. "We'll take a look inside. You were right in calling us. It's better to be safe than sorry."

The young cop returned within minutes. "Sir, we searched the house and there's no one inside. It probably was just a couple of kids out causing mischief, like you said. Next time you leave the house, make sure you lock up tight. Because the house was vacant for so long, those kids probably didn't know anyone lived here. Why don't you walk through and make sure nothing's been taken."

They walked throughout the house surveying its contents and condition. Nothing seemed out of the ordinary, other than their frayed nerves. Having the house broken into was the last thing they needed after the earlier conversation with Gus and the woman.

"Thank you officer, we feel much better knowing nothing was damaged. Does this sort of thing happen often around here?" asked Monique.

"No, can't say it does. Well folks you all have a great rest of the evening. Oh by the way, if you haven't already done so, I'd look into purchasing a security system. You'd be surprised how well they deter petty criminals."

"Yeah, I think we'll get that done right away. Thanks guys," stated Alphonse.

The police packed it all in and returned to their patrol cars, leaving the young couple to fend for themselves. They looked up and down the street at their neighbors peeking through slightly opened curtains.

"Would you look at them watching us?! What is wrong with these folks? Monique, I sure do hope we didn't make a mistake moving here. Come on you two, let's go inside."

CHAPTER FIVE

The end of summer arrived much too quickly. And as discussed during the neighborhood watch meeting, the residents of Greatview Island threw a magical celebration the weekend before Labor Day. Neighbors `who'd never spoken to one another ended up exchanging numbers and making arrangements to meet next year. Unfortunately, despite Monique and Alphonse's efforts to mingle, not one of their neighbors felt inclined to swap information.

They approached their next door neighbors, an older couple hanging out by the beer cooler, to inquire about their chickens.

"Hi, we haven't met yet, but we're your next door neighbors." Monique introduced herself.

"Hey, we've been meaning to get over to welcome you to the island, but it never seemed to be the right time. I'm Jerry and this is my wife Sue."

"So have you guys lived here for long? Did you know the previous owners?" asked Alphonse.

He observed Jerry's reaction of trying very hard not to react. The older man's blood seemed to drain from his face in a matter of moments. Sue also became visibly agitated at the question.

"It was nice meeting you both. I've got to finish packing because we're heading back to Wisconsin first thing tomorrow morning. Maybe we'll see you next year?"

"Oh? Nice meeting you, too," replied Monique. "Anyway Jerry, you were about to tell us about the previous owners."

"Listen, you seem like a nice enough couple and I don't want to frighten you with rumors. This is just our summer vacation home; we didn't get to know the other family before they moved. They were full timers on the island—like you. I don't know anything about the family other than they moved out shortly after they moved in. Folks around here said they never made it through the winter."

"We appreciate your honesty Jerry," said Alphonse. "So, tell me, what's the deal with the chickens?" he laughed.

Jerry stuttered when he spoke, "I-I-I'd get a few if I were you. You'll see what I mean if you stick around long enough. Well, it was nice meeting you folks." And just like that, he turned and walked away.

The next few weeks, they were almost used to having that side of the island all to themselves. The end of summer had for all intents and purposes effectively cut off all tourists visiting the island. Only the occasional police car passed by their house on its daily patrol.

*   *   *

"Monique, are you going to be alright here by yourself? I can see if I can postpone my trip or ask my mother to come out to stay with you."

"No, we'll be okay. I'm not going to let some scary ghost story keep me from enjoying our new home. You'll only be gone for a night anyway. And I am not going to run crying to your mother just because the weird people on this island are trying to freak me out."

"Okay, but if you need to call me or my family..."

"We'll be fine. Now go before you miss your plane."

"I love you." He kissed her goodbye. "Hey little man, you gonna protect your mother for me, alright?"

"I will Daddy. See you later." He hugged his father goodbye.

Monique and AJ stood on the sidewalk, waving as they watched Alphonse drive away. She looked up and down the street and immediately felt isolated. They were the only full time residents who remained on this side of the island. She knew if she really needed someone, there were other full timers in the older section, but they lived a couple of miles away. Good thing they purchased a golf cart to get around. However, knowing other people were on the island gave her little comfort because the last people she wanted to talk to were Gus and that old woman. They gave her the creeps.

"Well little man, it's just you and me. Wanna go to the beach?"

"Yay! We're going to the beach! Can I get in the water, Mommy?"

"Of course you can and I will join you. Let's go get changed."

Monique set the security alarm and put AJ to bed. Without Alphonse around, the house seemed much too big. She looked out the living room window and scanned the street. She observed nothing. No activity, no cars, no people taking late night walks. Her sense of isolation grew by leaps and bounds. When the house phone rang loudly, it startled her.

"Hello?" she answered.

"Hey Monique, how's my girl?" asked Alphonse.

"Doing okay. Just a little lonely, that's all. I just put AJ to bed and was about to turn in myself. I don't feel like watching television and I guess I'm bored as well. The house feels empty without you here."

"I know. I miss you too, but I'll be back tomorrow night. My flight arrives late and you'll probably be asleep by the time I make it home. Did you remember to set the alarm?"

"Yes, it's set. Hurry home baby."

"I'll try. I love you."

"Love you too. Goodnight," she replied.

"Goodnight."

After checking in on AJ one more time and leaving his door opened slightly, Monique settled down for the night with a romance novel. Because she usually went to sleep listening to Alphonse's light snoring, the bedroom was too quiet. She opened the bedroom window. The wind blew the curtains gently in the breeze. The sound of the waves proved to be soothing and she soon fell fast asleep.

In her erotic dream, Monique was approached by a handsome stranger. He lovingly stroked her hair and took her in his arms in an affectionate embrace. He picked her up and placed her gently on a bed resting on the beach. The man wept with joy as he kissed Monique from head to toe, savoring each piece of skin as if it were the first time he'd touched her. He kept repeating the words, 'I shall follow you to the ends of the earth', over and over again. And when he made love to her, all the worries of the world drifted away. She was at peace when her body convulsed in multiple orgasms.

"Mommy! Mommy! Mommy, wake up! You're scaring me Mommy!" cried AJ. He tried shaking his mother to wake her. He didn't like the strange way she was moaning. It frightened him and he started to cry.

Monique stirred and felt stuck in that unique place between wakefulness and dreaming. The handsome stranger had disappeared and was replaced by AJ standing beside her bed. She tried to wake up fully, but felt like she had been drugged. The pull to drift back asleep was powerful and she felt herself succumbing to the urge.

AJ started to scream, "Mommy! What's wrong Mommy?! Please wake up!" He continued to shake her, but she didn't budge. He remembered seeing a movie about throwing water in someone's face to wake them, so he ran to the bathroom and filled a paper cup with water. Walking with steadfast determination, he returned to the bedroom and poured the water over his mother's face.

Monique felt the water run down her neck and imagined it came from the beach scene from her dream. The pull to remain asleep grew faint.

She heard her son calling for his mother and she opened her eyes. AJ appeared terrified. His eyes were wide with fear and he was trembling.

"Baby, Mommy's okay. I'm fine. Don't cry." She pulled AJ into the bed and held him close. "Shhh, don't cry anymore, everything's going to be alright."

"Mommy, I was so scared. You were making a funny noise that woke me up so I came into your room. Your body was doing funny things and I got really scared."

Monique held her son tightly and continued to soothe him. She recalled the dream and imagined how good her dream lover made her feel. "It's alright. Don't cry anymore, Mommy's here. Go to sleep, my angel." She noticed how quiet the room was; the window was no longer open. "AJ, did you close my window?"

"No ma'am. I didn't," he answered half asleep.

That's strange, how did my window get closed? She looked around the bedroom and felt as if someone were watching. She left the lamp on and huddled underneath the covers with her son. In time, they both fell sound asleep.

Monique called Alphonse's mother the next day. She wanted to discuss last night with someone other than Alphonse. If she were to tell him what happened, he'd be on the first flight home. It wasn't that serious, yet she still wanted a sanity check.

"Hey Mom, can you stop by for coffee before your church meeting? You know how AJ loves his grandmother and I'd also like to see you."

"I'm sorry Monique. My car is in the shop, but you and AJ are more than welcome to stop by here."

"Okay, I'd like that. As soon as I get AJ dressed, we'll be on our way. See you soon, Mom."

Alphonse's mother pondered the urgency of Monique's request. She wondered if some other strange occurrence had happened in the house. She reviewed the information she and her husband Franklin obtained from the library about Greatview Island, particularly the story about the Redman family. *I can't show this to Monique when Alphonse is out of town, she'll never step foot in that house again. But on the other hand, how can I not tell her?*

"C'mon AJ, let's go! AJ? Where are you?" Monique searched AJ's room first, then the game room. He wasn't in either. She went downstairs to see if he was in the kitchen. When she saw the back door standing open, her heart practically stopped beating. She ran to the door and frantically called out, "AJ! AJ, where are you?!"

AJ was on the back deck looking at Sue and Jerry's backyard. "I'm over here Mommy. Look!

Something happened to the chickens." He pointed to a peculiar sight.

The yard was literally covered in feathers. Nary a chicken was in sight. She took AJ by the hand and walked to the other side of the deck and looked into her other neighbor's yard. More scattered feathers with no chickens.

"Let's go back inside." The early October morning was cool and she wore a light sweater. However, the chill she felt was not from the wind, but from what she'd just witnessed.

"Mother, I tell you something's strange going on inside the house. I don't want to sound paranoid, but it felt like someone was in my bedroom last night—watching me and AJ sleep. I went to bed with the window open and when I woke up, the window was closed."

"You probably just forgot you closed it earlier." She recalled the hideous image from the game room and visibly shuddered. "You not letting that child sleep in your bed, is you?"

"Not usually, but last night I had a nightmare and AJ had trouble waking me. We were both a little spooked, so I let him sleep in my bed." She sipped her coffee then told her the stories Gus provided. She also told her mother-in-law about the neighbor's chickens.

"What was the nightmare about?" asked her mother-in-law.

Monique blushed and replied, "Uh, well, actually it wasn't really a nightmare. I had an erotic dream and guess I got a little carried away. I woke up AJ."

"Oh? Erotic dream, huh? That's interesting…" she smirked and sipped her coffee.

"Yeah, it was actually very strange because I've never had one of those before."

"Seems like a lot of things are happening that haven't happened before." She looked at her daughter-in-law and asked, "Alphonse is coming home tonight? Right?"

Monique nodded. "He's getting in late, but he'll be here."

"Good, because I don't think it's wise leaving you two in that house by yourselves. Alphonse told me y'all is all alone in your neighborhood now. Did you know all them people left after summer was over when you moved there?"

"No Mother, we didn't know."

"Well, since Alphonse is coming back tonight, I want to show you something I discovered about the history of your house."

Monique held her hand up, "No need, we already know everything. We ran into a couple of older residents who happened to know all about the history of Greatview Island. They didn't leave anything out. Trust me. We know all about the slave graveyard, the Redman's, and how he committed suicide in the house."

"That don't bother you none?" she asked, incredulously.

"Not really, I don't believe in all that nonsense. There has got to be a rational explanation for what's been happening. It can't be all about spirits and ghosts."

"Well, as long as you know what you got yourself into, that's what matters. I was going to show you this file on the Redman's, but since you guys already know, I can toss it into the trash."

Monique caught a quick glimpse of a photograph lying on top of the stack. She gasped in shock and surprise. "Mother! That's the man from my dream last night! My dream lover!"

"Who? Him? Mr. Redman? This is the man you dreamt about?" Her mother-in-law looked closely at the picture Monique referred to. She had also seen this man before. Only not when he was alive. This was the man hanging from the beam in her son's game room. "Oh my!" she exclaimed.

Both women studied one another. Neither knew the right words to say to comfort the other.

Even Monique had to admit there was no explanation for her dream lover looking like the Mr. Redman. None that made sense anyway.

"I don't know what to do. Guess to be on the safe side, I'd better look into buying some chickens, huh?" Monique joked, nervously.

Her mother-in-law also wanted to ease the uncomfortable tension, "You may even think about getting a few pigs and goats while you're at it. If legend is true, that thing is going to get very hungry and a few chickens ain't gonna do a thing."

Both women laughed, hoping they'd still be laughing later on. Not wanting to be alone, Monique and AJ spent the major part of the day visiting with Alphonse's parents. It felt good to be with normal people again.

On the way home, Monique made a detour to the older section of the island in search of Gus. She remembered the general vicinity of where he lived, and considering not too many full-timers lived over there, he shouldn't be difficult to locate.

"Excuse me, I'm looking for Gus?" she asked a teenage girl out walking her dog.

"He lives at the end of the road in a big two story. Can't miss it. He has a huge orange and blue mermaid sitting in the front yard."

"Thanks!" She drove down the dirt road until she reached his house. *I'll be! It is a full-sized mermaid!* Gus sat outside his house in a lawn chair, puffing on a cigar.

"Well if it ain't the young lady from the wrong side of the tracks!" he joked.

She parked the car and helped AJ out. "Hi Gus, I hope I'm not disturbing you, but I need your help." She filled him in on the situation with the chickens.

"That seems to be quite a dilemma you have there, young lady. If you don't feed that thing, it'll go hunting for warm blooded animals and since you and your son are the closest living things around, it may make a direct move for you. On the other hand, if there's no live food available, maybe it'll go somewhere else looking for a meal." He reported in his matter of fact manner.

Monique involuntarily shuddered as she imaged a slimy marsh creature slinking up her backdoor, trying to get inside. "Maybe I should get a gun?" she asked aloud.

"Far as I know, guns ain't no good against this thing. It's alive, but it ain't, if you know what I mean. You can't kill nothin' that ain't really breathing." He blew a plume of cigar smoke upwards.

AJ listened intently at the adult conversation, not fully grasping the situation. He only knew his mother was scared, which scared him. He wanted his daddy to come home. So, not wanting to hear anything more about the people behind the fence he went to check out the mermaid.

"I can't believe I'm asking you this, but do you know where I can get some chickens?"

"Yep, I got a few in the back I can bring over later." He watched AJ play. "Where's your husband anyway?"

Monique contemplated lying, but figured the old man was harmless enough. "He was away on business, but he'll be back this evening."

"Okay, I'll bring them over later. You take care of your little boy and don't let him go wandering off—especially now that the weather's starting to turn."

"Thanks Gus, we'll see you later." Monique thought, *As soon as Alphonse returns we're going to buy a gun.*

CHAPTER SIX

"What do you mean you're not coming home tonight?!" Monique came close to losing control at the prospect of Alphonse being gone another night.

"I can't help it. There's supposed to be a bad storm brewing and we can't takeoff. All flights are cancelled for tonight, so I'm stuck in Chicago until possibly tomorrow. Have you watched the Weather Channel lately?"

"No, I haven't. Why? What's going on?" she asked, becoming alarmed.

"A nor'easter is headed your way tonight—straight towards Harperstown," he sighed.

They both thought about the story the old woman told them. It was during a nor'easter when the Redman family went missing. Of all days for Alphonse to be away, tonight was not the one for him to be gone.

"A nor'easter? Hold on for a minute. I'm going to check the weather." She turned to the local news. The breaking story was about the massive nor'easter headed their way. It was supposed to make landfall by ten o'clock that evening—only three hours away.

"Baby, I want you and AJ to stay at my mother's house tonight. I'll feel better and I know you will too if you're not there alone." He prayed Monique would not pick tonight to be stubborn. She surprised him with her response.

"Okay, you're right. I don't want to be stuck out here without you."

"That's my girl. Call me when you guys get to my parent's house. Give my little man a hug and kiss for me. I love you."

"Alphonse, hurry home," she replied before hanging up.

The doorbell rang about an hour later. Monique was in the midst of packing a suitcase for herself and arguing with AJ about not bringing every toy he had to his grandparent's. She looked out the door. It was Gus.

"Oh, hi Gus." She looked past him to his old truck. About a dozen chickens milled about in a cage. She couldn't believe she was going to put chickens in her backyard because of an island myth.

"Weather's turning bad. Looks like a big storm is headed our way. You sticking around for this one?" He looked and noticed Alphonse was still absent.

"No, we're going to my mother-in-law's to sit this one out. Since Alphonse won't be coming back, it's probably better for us to not be here alone. Considering…"

"Good decision because once the bridge floods, we're cutoff from the rest of Harperstown until the water recedes. Well, let me get these chickens set up and be on my way. I don't want to hold you up. That storms going to be here in the next thirty minutes or so."

"Thanks Gus. How much do I owe you?" She turned to get her purse.

"I'll settle up with your husband when he returns. You just get yourself and your child to a safe place. If you need me, here's my number." He scratched his phone number on a tiny piece of paper and handed it to her.

AJ watched Gus set up the chicken coop while Monique finished packing. She looked out the window when she heard his old truck sputter to life. They watched him drive off.

The wind picked up and the first heavy drops of rain began to fall. The tall grass of the marsh swayed in all directions as the wind furiously whipped it around. It was time to go.

Monique went to the garage and noticed the passenger door was accidently left open. She must've forgotten to close it earlier. She shut the car's door, loaded up the suitcases, and strapped AJ into his car seat. She opened the garage door to find that the sky had opened, pouring down buckets of rain. Strong gusts of wind blew trash down the street.

She turned the key. Whir, whir, whir, went the engine. Then nothing. She tried again. The car wouldn't start. "Damnit!" she screamed, pounding on the steering wheel. She let the car rest and tried again. Still nothing.

Monique got out of the car and popped the hood; not knowing what she was looking for she realized, *I need the battery jumped! Now where did I put Gus's number?* She fished around in her jean pockets trying to locate the tiny bit of paper. She found it, but the numbers were smudged and unreadable. She felt like crying until she looked at her son's face. He looked terrified.

"Mommy, what's wrong with the car?" He pulled his shirt into his mouth and started to chew furiously.

She realized she had to keep herself together for the sake of her child. "Hey baby, close the garage door for me. We're going to stay here tonight. At home."

AJ released the straps of his car seat and climbed across the front seat. He pressed the remote and the garage door slowly closed. Monique shut the hood and took her son inside.

"You want to play a game AJ? How about your *Wii*? That's always fun!"

He looked up at his mother with fear in his eyes. The howling wind and the loud rumbling of thunder scared him tremendously. "Yes, will you play with me?"

"Of course, I'm going to play with you. And guess what? We'll even play in the living room. Give me a minute to get it hooked up and then it's on, little dude!"

AJ liked it when his mother acted silly and called him *little dude*. Maybe it wouldn't be so bad after all being at home. He giggled and ran upstairs to his room to locate his favorite game. When he reached the top of the stairs, he heard that same voice calling out to him from the game room. He ignored it and went straight to his bedroom. Once he found the games, he quickly ran back down the stairs to his mother.

"How about frozen pizza for dinner? Does that sound good?" Monique wanted to allay her son's fears. She couldn't let on how she really felt because then they'd both be sniveling idiots.

So for the next couple of hours, they played all of AJ's favorite games and ate an entire pizza. And just about when it was time for bed, the phone rang. Monique answered.

"Hey, what are you guys still doing there?" asked Alphonse. "I thought you said you were going to my parent's house?"

"We were, but the car's battery died, so we're stuck at home. AJ and I are going to ride out our first nor'easter alone." She tried to sound brave, but Alphonse knew better.

"Damn! I wish I hadn't left you. I'm so sorry

Monique. If I had known about this storm, I would never have come on this trip. I feel so helpless!"

"We'll be fine." Monique didn't want to tell Alphonse about last night or the missing chickens. It would only add to his worry if he knew.

"AJ and I were just finishing up playing *Wii*. After I get him bathed and put to bed, I'll probably fall asleep watching some senseless movie."

"What's the weather like?"

"It sounds pretty bad out there! Lots of wind, rain, thunder and lightning. All in all, it's definitely a bad storm. Funny how these storms never bothered me before," she sighed.

"Before there never was a reason they should."

Monique had so much to tell him about her dream, the missing chickens, and his mother's discoveries. She decided saying nothing was better for now. No need to bother Alphonse when he a thousand miles away, stuck in an airport at the mercy of Mother Nature.

"I hope you make it out tomorrow. I can't wait to see you."

"Me too, baby. Me too. Go ahead and get little man to bed. I'll call you in the morning."

"Okay, we'll talk to you tomorrow. Goodnight."

She helped AJ with his bath and got him ready for bed. And after reading five different bedtime stories, he finally fell asleep. She left the hallway light on and his door open just a tiny bit.

Monique was only slightly concerned about a replay of last night's strange events. But this time before turning in, she made certain all the doors and windows were securely locked then activated the security alarm. And for added security, she pushed a heavy bookcase in front of the back door, just in case little AJ got up in the middle of the night. Before she went upstairs, she turned on the back porch light. There was some water in the yard, but not enough to be concerned about. So with a sigh of relief, she climbed the stairs and checked on AJ once more before going to bed.

Just like last night, Monique was visited in her sleep by her dream lover. Knowing who he was didn't make her feel any differently. She wasn't afraid, for he was tender, loving, and kind. He spoke to her and said he would protect her and her child. Once again he made love to Monique over and over again.

When she awoke in the middle of night, she was totally naked and covered in perspiration. She wondered, *Was he actually here? Impossible! How can a ghost make love to a real woman? And how did my nightgown get removed without my knowing?* Her body felt as if she had been physically touched—aggressively made love to. She got up and showered, feeling dirty and ashamed of how her body betrayed her.

The storm continued on through the night. When Monique awoke late the next morning, AJ was already up. She went into his room and he wasn't there. With a mother's instinct, she intuitively knew where he was—downstairs staring out the window as if he were hypnotized. When she looked into the backyard, she was glad she had the foresight to block the door with the bookcase. The dirty murky water was almost to the top of the deck. She cried out in horror when she saw fluffy white feathers floating on top. It must be true. The marsh had come into her back yard bringing with it some ancient horrible creature. It had eaten the chickens and would soon be back for more.

"Mommy, why did you block the door? My friends wanted me to come out to play?" AJ said in a strange voice.

"Baby, what are you talking about? There's nothing out there but water."

"Uh uh Mommy. It's in the water. I saw it get the chickens."

"What did you see AJ?" she asked, feeling as if she were going to pass out.

He whispered, "I saw a monster come out of the water. It wanted me to come out to play, but I couldn't get the door open. It tried to get in, but it couldn't. So it took the chickens and went back into the water. I was really scared."

Oh my God! We've got to get out of here! Monique ran to the front of the house and saw water from the ocean gushing down the street. "C'mon baby, we're going to go for a walk. Let's get you dressed."

She quickly dressed her son in his raincoat and galoshes. She had no raingear so she pulled on a pair of Alphonse's workpants and boots. As she unlatched the front door, the wind whipped the screen door wide open, breaking the glass. She picked up AJ and tried walking on the sidewalk. The water in the street must've been at least a foot deep at its shallowest point. They made it only as far as the intersection. At that point, the water converged into a swirling whirlpool and she couldn't see the bottom of the road.

There was no way she could navigate across the road safely carrying AJ and even if she did, Gus lived at least another mile away. In resigned defeat, she turned back to her house. Today when she looked at the house on Lakeview, she didn't see a dream home, but instead it turned into a living nightmare.

"AJ, I want you to stay away from the windows. And whatever you do, don't look into the marsh! I don't want you speaking to anything I can't see. *I had no idea what he saw earlier, but I didn't want to take any chances.*

"Yes ma'am. But what about the man upstairs? What do I do when he talks to me? He was nice and stopped the monster from getting in."

Monique dropped the dish she was drying in the sink. It shattered. The hairs on the back of her neck stood up. "A man upstairs? What man?" She held her breath waiting for him to explain.

"The man in the game room. He talks to me sometimes and tells me to not be scared. He said he's here to protect us." AJ played with his action figures as if everything were normal.

Monique listened to her son, trying her best to remain calm. Every fiber in her being screamed for her to get out of the house—grab her son and get away from the impending doom that was certain to come. Yet, she was trapped in the very house she fought so hard to get.

"AJ, what did the man look like?"

"I don't know. He was just a man. Kinda like Daddy but with more hair. His eyes looked really weird."

It had to be Redman. Like the photo her mother-in-law showed to her, Redman sported an afro, just like her dream lover. Monique looked out the kitchen window at the tall grass of the marsh. The way the grass frantically swayed back and forth, it appeared something was alive in there and trying to get out. She thought, *I can't let my imagination get the best of me! Got to stay calm.* The rain had let up some, but the murky marsh water was now level to the deck. She had no idea if the water would continue to rise and make its way into the house. She prayed it would not.

Ring, ring, ring went the phone. In the quiet of the house, the loud piercing noise always managed to make her jump in fright.

"AJ, turn on the television while I get the phone."

"Okay Mommy." He picked up the remote and tuned in the *Cartoon Network.*

"Hello?" she answered.

"Monique, what happened? Alphonse said you were supposed to be coming here last night." asked her mother-in-law.

"I'm sorry Mom, but with everything going on, I forgot to call to say we weren't going to make it. The car's battery died so we're stuck on the island."

"Oh no! That's awful! I got worried when I didn't hear from you. Both me and Alphonse have been trying to reach you guys since last night. I was starting to think your phone was off."

"No, the phone is working just fine; we didn't lose electricity either."

"That's strange, our calls wouldn't go through. Anyway, Alphonse called me this morning. He wanted me to call you and tell you that his flight got out. He's on his way home."

"Thank God!"

"Is everything else okay…?"

Understanding what her mother-in-law asked, she replied, "I think he visited me again last night—in my dreams," she paused. "I put chickens in the backyard yesterday…they're gone now. And the water is almost at the deck… Mom, AJ said he saw a monster this morning."

"Baby, get out of the house! Go anywhere! I don't think it's safe for you guys there anymore!"

"I've already tried. The water's too deep and the streets are practically impassable. We don't have a choice. We have to stay here," replied Monique, resigned to her fate.

"Lord have mercy! I don't know what to tell you other than to pray. Pray like you've never prayed before. I'll be doing the same for you. Me and Poppa will try our best to get to you, but until then stay strong."

"Thanks Mom. Please hurry!"

"Mommy! Mommy! Look!" screamed AJ.

"I've got to go, AJ's calling me."

"Okay, I'll see you soon. *I hope*."

Monique replaced the phone on the hook. The temperature in the room seemed to drop to freezing in the span of a moment. Her breathing quickened allowing her to see the vapors of her own breath.

She felt its presence before she actually saw it. She turned around and inhaled sharply. The apparition before her was definitely the man from the photo—the man from her dream. His form seemed solid, yet transparent at the same time. His eyes were grotesque and bugged out. His deformed tongue prevented him from speaking; that is if it could. He raised his arm and pointed to the kitchen where her son screamed for her. It seemed to levitate and quickly disappeared.

AJ promised his mother he wouldn't look outside, but the scraping sound at the window was too much to resist. He tiptoed to the window and pulled back the drapes. The thing had no particular shape and appeared to be formed from water, rotten vegetation, and snakes. It raised its appendage and clawed at the glass trying to get in. AJ let the curtain go and screamed for his mother.

Monique ran to her son and pulled him away from the window. She too heard the awful scraping sound, but was too afraid to see what it was. What she observed next caused her to scream out in horror. The apparition of the man reappeared and changed into something truly horrific right in front of their eyes. It made a horrendous snarling, growling noise and passed straight through the wall. The sound of ferocious animals fighting went on for several minutes before finally subsiding. Only when she was sure that whatever was out there was gone, did she pull back the curtain. The deck was now fully submerged in the murky water. Clumps of rotted weeds, interspersed with various species of snakes swirled around what once was the deck.

"Mommy, I'm scared!" cried AJ.

"Me too, baby. Me too."

CHAPTER SEVEN

Hours later, the storm finally seemed to subside and the howling winds died down. Once again, Monique bundled AJ up in his raingear to see if the roads were passable. Although the ocean water no longer poured from the beach, the water was still too deep to wade across. They had no choice but to return to the house.

Monique's cell phone vibrated loudly from inside her purse. She'd left it there from yesterday when she and AJ tried to leave the island. After she fished it out, she saw there were several missed calls from Alphonse and his mother.

"Hey sweetheart," she answered.

"Thank goodness you're alright! I was so worried when I couldn't reach you on the house phone. Is it out of service?"

"No, the phone's okay, but with the way the weather's been acting there's no telling. So are you in town yet?" She was so happy to hear his voice.

"Yes, I just landed. Do you know what the roads are like?"

"I can imagine they're flooded, considering what our backyard looks like." She didn't want to go into further detail about earlier events.

"What do you mean? Is it flooded?"

"Up to the back door!" she exclaimed. "But the storm appears to be letting up so hopefully it will go down soon."

"Yeah, it's high tide now. When the tide recedes, so should the water." He recalled Gus's conversation. "Hey, by the way, anything strange happen since I've been away?"

Monique decided to come clean with her husband. "Since you asked…" And for the next thirty minutes she filled Alphonse in on everything—including the chickens, the ghost, AJ's conversations, and the marsh creature. While doing so, she kept a close eye on her son. So far, the apparition had not appeared again.

"I want you to try to make it to Gus's house where you and AJ will be safe until I can reach you. I'll be there as soon as I can, my love."

"Alphonse, please hurry."

By nightfall, the storm had fully passed and in the clear night sky, the stars were out in full force. Monique checked the streets again. Since the water was no longer flowing, she bundled up her son and carried him into the night. With flashlight in hand, she waded in the water knee deep trying to get to the other side of the island. Suddenly she felt something slither past her legs. She shined the flashlight down into the water and saw they were surrounded by snakes.

"Oh shit!" she whispered, realizing any sudden movement could cause the creatures to grasp onto her and sink their poisonous fangs deep into her flesh—then her son's. Mustering up all the calmness she could, she gradually waded out of the water and back to her house. Seemed like no matter how much she tried, the house or whatever was in it, wouldn't allow their escape.

"Mommy, is Daddy coming home tonight? I'm real scared and I don't want to sleep in my room. The boogie man might get in the house and take me away." And for the first time since all this had started, her little man broke down and cried little boy tears.

"Yes baby, Daddy will be home tonight. *At least I hope he will!* He's going to come get us and take us away from here. I promise. We just have to be brave and make it through tonight. Okay? Now, let's get you dried off and put to bed."

Once again, she secured the downstairs doors and windows and set the alarm before heading upstairs. Monique spent the majority of the night in AJ's room reading him bedtime stories and singing lullabies. When she was sure he was sound asleep, she decided to take a nice warm bubble bath before turning in.

Monique dreamt Alphonse had finally returned and climbed into their bed. He stroked her body and told her how much he missed and loved her and his child. He said he would never let anything hurt them again. He was there to protect her. She loved how gentle he was and the tenderness he displayed making love to her. Monique's body reacted to his in perfect harmony. As if they were made for one another. Her moans of ecstasy stirred not only her dream lover, but also the creature that awaited its next meal.

* * *

Alphonse called his father from the airport and asked to borrow his old motorboat. He couldn't let his family stay in that house another night.

His father picked up his son and drove over to the dock to get the boat. When he was halfway to Greatview Island, they had to stop. The road was flooded and the bridge was down, literally cutting off all access to the island. Alphonse's father hoisted the boat into the water and started the motor. He prayed his son would be okay and able to rescue his family.

"I'll be here waiting when you return son. Now go get your family!"

"Thanks Pop!" He hugged his father and hopped into the boat. And under the darkness of a moonless night, Alphonse steered the boat into the marsh. He was amazed at the depth of the standing water, yet navigated around the numerous obstacles the storm had strewn about.

His family was in danger and it was up to him to rescue them!

Somehow, he managed to locate his house. He tied the boat to a lamp post and waded through the water to the front steps. It was late and all the lights in the house were out. He opened the door and disengaged the security system. The beep, beep, beep sound temporarily reassured him of his sanity.

Alphonse reset the alarm and climbed the stairs two at a time. The hallway lights were on—probably as a safety precaution for AJ. He heard a gentle moaning sound coming from his bedroom. He smiled, relieved, and imagined Monique was simply having a nightmare. He decided to sneak in under the covers and surprise his wife. He opened the door slightly and peeked inside. Alphonse was horrified at the sight that greeted him.

Monique *was* moaning in her sleep alright, but not because of a nightmare. He approached the bed and watched the dreadful sight unfold in front of his eyes. The ghost or whatever it was,

was in the midst of making love to his wife. It looked up at him with hideous yellow eyes and grinned, exposing sharp rotten teeth. The man's tongue hung grotesquely from the side of its mouth when he bent down to kiss Monique. Alphonse watched in horror as Monique arched her back and wrapped her arms around the dead thing's head. She screamed out Alphonse's name as the creature brought her to climax.

"Get off my wife!" Alphonse jumped at the ghost of Redman and ended up on top of Monique instead.

She awoke, startled and confused from her erotic dream and pulled a sheet over her body to cover her nakedness. "Alphonse, baby you're home!" She went to wrap her arms around her husband, but was taken aback when he rolled off the bed.

"Monique? What the fuck is going on?!" he yelled.

And at the very moment, they heard glass breaking downstairs. The alarm blared in response to the break in the security barrier.

Alphonse ran to the bureau, pulled out a pair of sweats and tossed them to his wife. Explanations for what he'd witnessed would have to come later. For now, they needed to get the hell out of there. "Get dressed!"

Monique, still half asleep, didn't totally

comprehend what had just occurred. One moment she was dreaming about making mad, passionate love to her husband, and the next he was standing in the bedroom screaming at her to get dressed. "Alphonse, what's the matter?!" she asked.

Hearing the commotion coming from both downstairs and his parent's bedroom, AJ went to investigate. He crept down the hallway and stood at the top of the stairs. The thing called out his name disguised as his mother's voice. AJ groggily descended the stairs to find his mother.

"Quiet! Did you hear that?! I think AJ's up!" He listened to the voices coming from downstairs. "Oh my God, it's calling AJ! Monique! Get your ass in gear so we can get our son and get out of here!"

He ran from the bedroom and down the stairs two at a time. "AJ? AJ?! Where are you son?!" he yelled, frantically running from room to room. Alphonse stopped when he reached the kitchen. The French doors were broken from the outside in. Glass was everywhere. Yet, AJ was nowhere to be found.

Monique turned off the alarm because she knew no police would respond. "Did you find him?" she shouted as she ran into the kitchen.

"No, I didn't! Oh my God?! Where is my

son?!" Alphonse stressed as he looked all over the bottom floor.

Monique felt compelled to look out the kitchen window towards the marsh. She screamed when she saw her son wrapped in the arms, appendages, tentacles, of whatever the creature was suspended at least ten feet above the water. AJ frantically tried to get free, yet the more he struggled, the tighter the thing clamped down.

"Baby, what is it?! Did you find him?!" Alphonse ran to his wife's side, out of breath. When she didn't answer, he turned his focus to where her gaze resided.

"Holy shit!" he exclaimed, looking out the window.

Alphonse ran to the back door and stepped into the deep water covering the deck. He treaded water to get to the thing and inadvertently stepped off the deck into the yard. He immediately went underneath because the water had to be at least six feet deep. There was no way to reach AJ.

Monique screamed out, "Please give him back to me! He's just a little boy and he didn't do anything wrong. Please give me my baby back!" She felt totally helpless watching her little boy be dragged kicking and screaming into the marsh.

Out of nowhere, she felt the familiar coldness

surround her. The apparition of Redman appeared at her side. First it looked at her, then at Alphonse struggling in the water, and finally it rested its gaze upon AJ fighting the creature's grasp. In that moment, she finally understood everything. The ghost had somehow confused her and AJ with its missing family. They represented the family Redman had lost to the creature in the marsh.

It bent its deformed face towards her and kissed her on the cheek. Monique fought the urge to vomit and allowed the ghost to kiss her. Then just as before, it transformed its shape to resemble a monster that looked like it came straight from hell. It made a horrible sound and went after the marsh creature. The thing dropped AJ into the water. Alphonse swam over to his son and pulled him safely to the deck.

Alphonse grabbed Monique by the arm and pulled her out the front door. He placed his family in the small motorboat and sped away. They turned and looked backwards at their dream home. And in the backyard over the marsh, a strong storm reappeared. A bolt of lightning flashed from the sky and made a direct hit on their house. A huge fireball erupted and flames quickly spread from their home to the next, and the next, and on and on...

* * *

"Yes siree! That was the damndest thing I have ever witnessed in my eighty plus years on this earth! Greatview Island went up in flames that night. Looked like Armageddon had erupted over there. And weren't a damned thing none of us could do. Couldn't no fire engines get passed because of the roads being flooded. I'm just happy that nice family escaped unharmed. Yes indeed." Gus shook his head and popped an unlit cigar in his mouth.

"Let me ask you Mr. Redman, does your family have any intention of rebuilding?" asked the female newscaster.

Gus shrugged his shoulders, turned and walked back to his home. In his heart of hearts, he was pleased to finally be free of the entire mess. *Good riddance to it all!*

"That was an eyewitness account from Gus Redman of the largest fire in Harperstown's history. At least one hundred homes were destroyed as a result of the nor'easter. Luckily, most of these homes were vacation homes and vacant at the time. Amazingly no one got hurt. Now, back to you Bob." The newscaster signaled "cut" to her camera man. They packed up the news van, thanked Gus for his time, and left in search of the next breaking news story.

THE END

OYA – THE CHOSEN ONES

CHAPTER 1

"Jerald! Don't you dare!" shouted Marcella, at the top of her lungs just as the kickball left the boy's hands. Too late! The children watched to see if the ball would hit its intended target. *It is too hot to be out here! And would you look at this little…*

The red kickball sailed past the little girl's thick braids, held precariously together by a single yellow barrette. It barely missed the small pink tongue protruding from her mouth, stuck out in victory at the boy's mistaken throw. Her hands went to her hips as she sang out, "Na na na na na!"

Marcella monitored the kickball game from the sidelines, blowing her whistle every now and then just to let the class know she was still paying attention. The preteen boys, full of youthful energy, had secretly begun a contest to see who could successfully bounce the kickball from their female classmate's heads and not get caught by the teacher. They didn't know she knew.

Bill Fletcher, the sixth grade music teacher, always seemed to have too much time on his hands. At least once a day, he found his way to the soccer field to blow off steam, usually about something involving their boss. Since Marcella was fairly new to the school, he hoped to find an ally in dissing the principal. So far, it hadn't worked.

Marcella tucked her long micro braids into a ponytail holder to get the hair off her neck— desperately trying to cool off. She pulled a handkerchief from her back pocket and dabbed her forehead dry. It wasn't even nine o'clock, yet the hot sun unmercifully beat down adding to her increasing irritability with the children's behavior. She also had enough of Bill's callous comments about Mr. Jones. Unfortunately, her mirrored sunglasses blocked Bill from seeing the growing annoyance in her eyes.

It had been only a month since she accepted the job as a gym teacher. Having recently graduated with a degree in physical therapy, it was the only job she could find in the small seaside community of Solstice that paid more than minimum wage. Newly hired teachers were placed on probation their first year and she wanted to make a good impression with her boss. Being seen chatting with the music teacher on a regular basis wouldn't look good on her quarterly review.

All of a sudden, the ground shifted beneath

their feet. "Whoa! Did you feel that?!" asked Bill, steadying himself as the ground lurched violently. Reflexively his arms reached towards Marcella to catch her fall.

"Yeah... What *was* that?!" Marcella asked, momentarily shaken. She held onto Bill's arm to keep from falling.

An unexpected strong gust of wind and an ear shattering noise, that seemed to come from the sky, directly followed the earth's movement as if the events were somehow connected. The children's attention first turned towards the direction of the sound; then became focused on the teachers.

"Miss Butler?! Was that an earthquake?! What was that loud sound?! Maybe something exploded! Did you feel that wind?! It came out of nowhere and almost knocked me over!" exclaimed Jerald, running over to the adults out of breath.

"I don't know Jerald. Stay here!" instructed Marcella, as she headed towards the teacher's aide running towards her.

With one hand holding the whistle securely between her teeth, the teacher's aide wildly waved her free hand trying to get Marcella's attention. She frantically blew the whistle and motioned for the class to get off the field.

* * *

"Fire! Fire! Fire!" screamed Liz from the top of her lungs. "Gather the children outside! Now!" She rushed up and down the school's narrow hallway shouting out instructions to all within earshot. The fire alarm blared loudly in the background.

Though there was no actual fire, she knew of no other way to get everyone's attention quickly, so shouting "Fire!" was a sure way to do it. Liz knew without being told that today was going to end badly. She suspected this was the day the town had prepared for, but hoped would never arrive.

Practically every school had someone who has been around so long they literally become part of the institution. For thirty-eight years, Elizabeth "Liz" Rose was that person. As head secretary, Liz had survived at least a dozen principals—saw them come; watched them go.

At 67 years of age, Liz was the "go to" person when the children needed someone to talk to. Due to her age, her family made no bones about wanting Liz to stop working and start enjoying her retirement years, but she would not acquiesce. She loved working and said that's what kept her young. Anytime anyone asked her why she kept working, she proudly responded, "It's my life's mission to keep the children safe."

Mrs. Hernandez's first grade class was in the middle of saying the pledge of allegiance when the loud noise abruptly interrupted their daily morning ritual. The single jolt that followed afterwards, shaking her classroom, didn't raise any immediate concerns. Being so close to the mountains, Solstice naturally experienced small earthquakes on a regular basis. No big deal, the earthquake probably accidently set off the fire alarm.

She heard Liz in the hallway screaming out "Fire!" *That's odd. Why is Elizabeth behaving so strangely? It isn't like her to be frantic*, Mrs. Hernandez thought. *After all, it's just a fire alarm*. She stuck her head out the door to quietly speak with the secretary for the briefest of moments. After confirming the situation with Liz, Mrs. Hernandez returned to her classroom and nervously picked up her cell phone. She excused herself to the back of the room to phone her husband.

As she was about to hit the call button, her cell phone rang. She looked at the caller ID and saw that it was her husband. "I was just about to call you, honey. What happened? What's going on out there? They're saying it wasn't just an earthquake."

Mr. Hernandez replied, "Hey sweetie. Are you alright? I'm not sure what's going on either.

One minute I was waiting on a customer when all of a sudden I heard a very loud boom! The building started to shake and stuff starting falling off the shelves. The noise shattered most of the storefront windows on Main Street. Everyone here is in a panic," he explained nervously. He offered no further explanation, for he had none.

"I just spoke to Elizabeth. Nobody knows if this is really *it* and I'm sort of s-s-scared..." she replied. But she never got the opportunity to complete her thoughts. The last thing she heard before the line went dead was, "Honey, I love you".

Minutes later, she stood in front of her classroom and said in as calm a voice as she could muster, "Children, I need for you to remain calm. Okay? Please get your backpacks off the hooks and line up like we always do for a fire drill. Remember, no pushing and no running."

The first graders obediently lined up alphabetically, as if preparing to leave their classrooms for lunch or a recess break. Though they were nervous, the only way an onlooker could tell something was amiss was the unusual lack of chatter. As a matter-of-fact the children were uncommonly quiet. Twenty-two six and seven year olds, normally full of exuberant boundless energy, stood unusually still.

The school practiced fire drills at least once a month, anticipating the day when this day would finally come—that day was here. The children followed their teacher's instructions to the letter. They calmly trailed behind the class leader out the door, down the hall and across the parking lot to the designated meeting place under the tall oak tree. Other classes did the same.

"No, not outside! Get in here! Now! Go to the basement! Take the children down to the basement! Quickly!" Mr. Jones screamed, seeming to come out of nowhere.

"But, sir it's only a fire drill," stated one of the teacher's aides rolling her eyes at the principal. "We don't stay indoors for a fire drill. Our usual meeting place is here—under the big shade tree."

"Listen to me! This is no time for questions. Do as I say and do it quickly!" Mr. Jones tried to remain calm, although the perspiration dripping from his brow and the dark armpit stains forming on his shirt betrayed his emotions. He took one look at the woman barely out of her teens and thought, *what in the world makes this child think she knows better than I do?!*

Reginald Jones was unremarkable in every way that mattered. He grew up in Solstice, never wanting to live anywhere else. He hadn't married and had fathered no children. A runner by nature, his 5'10" frame remained fit and trim. Friends used to tease him by saying he could blend into a crowd and easily get lost, for his caramel brown skin, receding hairline, and black framed glasses made him nondescript—almost invisible. In his mid 50's, his life was first dedicated to being a teacher, and now as the principal. The faculty and the children were his family. They were all he had and all he ever needed.

"I'm sorry sir! I didn't think it was that serious. Come on kids, follow me," replied the aide upon seeing the desperation on the principal's face. She quickly ushered the children back into the building.

CHAPTER 2

As if on cue, a thunderstorm formed quickly in the once blue sky. The emergency warning sirens switched on, morphing the first day of spring into the makings of a nightmare. The wind picked up blowing tender white spring blossoms resembling heavy snowflakes into the air. The temperature dropped from the mid 80's to barely above freezing in less than a minute. Rolling thunder that sounded like angels bowling was followed by electrifying cloud-to-cloud lightning. In fact, the air was so highly charged they felt the hairs on the back of their necks prickle.

"Mr. Jones?" asked Marcella, in a tiny frightened voice. "What the hell is going on?" The fear she saw lurking behind his eyes, buried under a confident façade, alarmed her more than anything else.

"To be perfectly honest Miss Butler, we're still trying to figure it out. I received a call from the school superintendent right before the sirens started. He told me to gather all the students and take shelter in the basement. Something having to do with this storm. Right now, I'm waiting for his call." He used the back of his hand to wipe away the cold sweat running down his face.

Nearly 150 students and teachers managed to squeeze into the basement's storage room. A few younger children cried for their parents. The older students thought it was cool to skip class and catch up with their friends.

Several teachers huddled together in a corner, nervously speculating about the chain of events. Others pulled out their cell phones, trying to get enough bars to make a call—to contact their loved ones in town. It was futile, because even on the best days the signal was very weak. And deep within the confines of the school basement's concrete foundation, picking up a cell phone signal was virtually impossible. The group was literally cut off from the world.

The old wall mounted phone rang out in a high shrill tone. As everyone's nerves were on edge, they all jumped at the unfamiliar sound. It had been a long time since any one heard, much less used, a land based line.

"Um, excuse me Miss Butler, that's probably him now." Mr. Jones dusted off the emergency land line, a relic left over from way back when—before cell phones became popular. He spoke in hushed tones.

The room grew quiet enough to hear the shallow breathing of the frightened children. The other adults tried to listen in, hoping to gauge the conversation from the principal's reaction. He gave nothing away with his facial expressions—just nodded his head and muttered in monosyllable responses. He knew all eyes *and* ears were on him and any hint of his being alarmed could send everyone into chaos.

"Yes, yes, uh huh, I understand. Yes, sir, will do. Okay. Right, right, right. That seems to be the best way. I'll let them know. No, sir, I won't let that happen. They're fine. Yes, I understand sir. Good-bye." He hung up the phone and cleared his throat, stalling to find the right words. It was quiet enough to hear a pin drop.

"Children, first of all thank you for being so patient. I want you to know you are safe here, so don't be worried. We'll get you out of here and back to your parents as quickly as we can. But for now, being down here in the school's basement is the safest place for you—for all of us." He attempted a reassuring smile that came out half-hearted.

"Mr. Fletcher, Miss Butler, Mrs. Hernandez would you please join me over here, in private?" He huddled the group into a corner while the aides played games with the children. Games meant to distract their attention from the very worried and frightened adults.

"Reggie, w-w-what is it? Are they here?" Elizabeth asked, in hushed tones.

Mr. Jones sighed heavily, "Yes Liz, I think it's finally happening. God help us all! The superintendent has no idea what we're dealing with, but I think *this* is it. What *we've* been waiting for all these years.... Listen up! We've got to remain calm and keep the children quiet. I think we're safe down here—for now."

The elderly woman didn't look frightened; she appeared resigned to deal with the hand they were dealt. She dropped her head and studied her hands.

"Bill, I need you to go with me and make sure all the outside doors are locked. We've got to make it look like this place is abandoned. Ladies, gather up as much food as you can. We don't know how long this is going to last. Make the children comfortable. Keep them busy. Most importantly, keep them quiet! I'm sure most of their parents have already prepared them for the day. They'll have questions, but don't be too specific in your answers if you can help it. The superintendent says he'll give me a call when he knows more. For now, let's do what we can. You guys up for this?" He surveyed the group and they all nodded in agreement—everyone that is, except Marcella.

"I'm sorry sir, but I still don't understand. What's going on? *What* has finally happened? Why is everyone so scared? And why are we hiding in the basement?" asked Marcella, noting willowy cobwebs and insect skeletons scattered about the floor.

"That's right; you're not originally from here. Come upstairs with me and Bill and I'll explain as much as I can while we secure the school. Mrs. Hernandez, you're in charge 'til we get back."

* * *

Marcella trailed closely behind the two men and discreetly slipped out the crowded room. The children were occupied so their departure went unnoticed. Marcella heard the bolt lock click smoothly back into place behind them.

The group of three took the short flight of stairs up to the main level. The school was eerily quiet. Too quiet for her taste. Her expensive sneakers squeaked noisily on the highly polished floors. One by one, they secured all classrooms on both floors, ensuring all windows were locked and blinds lowered. The double doors leading outside were held tight by heavy padlocked linked chains. Following Mr. Jones's directions, lights were turned off, computers powered down, and appliances were disconnected from electrical outlets.

"Okay, we've secured the school. Now can you please fill me in on what's going on? All this is very strange. We're acting like we're hiding from someone. Or something. What was that loud noise I heard earlier before the sirens kicked off?"

"Look Marcella, I know you want answers, but we had to secure the school first." He mopped his damp forehead with a handkerchief. "Follow me to my office. I want to show you both something. You too, Bill." Mr. Jones turned on the overhead light.

He pulled the custom made leather chair to his desk and turned on the computer. The familiar sound of *Microsoft Windows* coming to life was oddly comforting because it remained consistent when everything else around them seemed surreal.

By now the sky was fully overcast—almost dark, though it couldn't have been later than noon. The howling wind temporarily masked the wailing noise coming from the warning sirens. The entire scene resembled something from a bad horror movie. Only it wasn't a movie. It was real.

"While the computer is booting, I want to tell you a story. A somewhat forgotten history of Solstice, our *cozy* little community." He sat back in his seat and sighed, "We won't be here very long, but might as well get comfortable."

"When I was just a little boy, probably around 5 or 6, my great-grandfather Papa Leroy used to tell me stories about this town. About Solstice. Stories that were passed down through the generations—ones that started back before Solstice was even a town. Did you know that the cemetery next to the school was once used as a place to burn woman believed to be witches? Later on they started burying slaves there—since it was already *tainted*." He referred to the small plot of land next to the play ground.

"My wife has some kin buried over there. So what?" Bill interjected.

Mr. Jones ignored Bill's comment and continued. "Most of the cemetery caretakers have either died off or moved away. Now it's become an overgrown thicket of weeds, shrubs and poison ivy. No one visits there anymore. Every now and then a church will volunteer to come clean up the place—get rid of overgrown weeds. They tend to the old headstones of the original inhabitants."

Marcella shrugged also hoping he would get to the point of his story.

"If we make it through today, I'll take you over for a look. You'll probably recognize some of the names on the headstones as your ancestors, too."

"Anyway, everybody told me not to pay my

great-grandpa no mind because he was showing signs of Alzheimer's. Back then, they used to call it *going senile*. Papa Leroy would sit outside my grandma's house and talk to himself. All day long, he'd sit in that worn out rocking chair having a good old time laughing and carrying on. Being so young, I didn't know any better. So one day I got brave and I asked him who was he talking to. He looked me squarely in the eye and plain as day told me he was speaking to his wife who passed away years earlier."

Bill Fletcher's posture relayed his annoyance with hearing the often repeated familiar story yet again. He sighed and muttered under his breath, "Oh boy, here we go again!"

"Papa Leroy said, *'Since everybody thinks I'm crazy anyhow, why not have a good time and pretend she's still here?'* Well, I got a kick from being let in on his secret. So the summer before he passed, I spent every single day at his knee listening to him carry on, telling fantastic stories from his past. Listening to Papa Leroy was way better than watching TV. I discovered he wasn't crazy, just lonely." His eyes misted over at the memory.

Marcella smiled thinking of her own grandparents, who lived just a few miles away. When this was over—if this was over, she was going to make a point to visit them.

"I remember the day he first told me about the *others* because it seems like it was just yesterday. He confided there was something different about some of the town's people. Said they were *Chosen Ones* placed here long ago by God to keep an eye on the rest of us; to protect us from the bad spirits that would eventually come. Chosen Ones are said to be similar to angels, but they lived amongst us and looked just like normal folks. He told me some of them didn't know they were special. Just went about their business living normal lives and raising families like the rest of us."

Bill Fletcher added, "Yeah, I remember listening to my parents speak about them growing up. *Funny what you remember from your childhood.* The old people simply called them *Oya*—meaning spirits of the wind and rain. I never did put much stock in those old stories. Nothing more than fairy tales, if you ask me."

"You have a right to your opinion Bill," Mr. Jones continued, "Oya have something more than regular folks—like an extra chromosome or something. An Oya will give you the shirt off their backs, even if it's the only shirt they own. You'd think most of would be church going folks, but that isn't always the case. In fact, some of the preachers, pastors, and church leaders are not Oya—some are, but most aren't. Papa Leroy thought that was hilarious and that's why he gave up on organized religion. Thought it was sinful to put faith in men who weren't really called on by God to serve." He punched in his password and waited for the screen to pop up.

"He told me all this because he suspected I might be an Oya. Always said he saw something special in me—that I was different from my brothers and sisters. Before Papa Leroy passed, he proclaimed that I was destined to be somebody great. I had no idea what he meant at the time, just knew that I loved Papa Leroy with all my heart. To this day, I can't say his prophecy came true. After all, I'm just an elementary school principal in a tiny black community. We're barely on the map." Mr. Jones shrugged off the possibility of being anything more than what he was.

Bill Fletcher secretly despised Mr. Jones. He believed the principal was too arrogant to be anyone's *Chosen One. There's no way in hell that man could be an Oya—not the Oya my parent's believed in. He's something, but an Oya ain't it!*

"Papa Leroy predicted one day the evil ones would come forth one day to reign terror on this earth and only the Oya could stop them. Said the evil ones come to poison people's hearts and minds and spread mayhem everywhere they go.

They would arrive on a day like today, on a gust of wind as strong as a tornado, accompanied by a tremendous noise. Possibly the noise would be as loud as breaking the sound barrier—a sonic boom. We've awaited and prepared ourselves for this day. Of course we have our skeptics, but deep down I think everyone believes."

"Well, now that does sound crazy! Who in their right mind believes in that superstition? It sounds like old wives tales and foolishness. Angels? Chosen ones? Oya? Evil forces taking over? What in the world?!" exclaimed Marcella, rolling her eyes upwards.

"Marcella, you're not from here, but I know your people are. You even have ancestors buried over there—in that cemetery. Why else would you choose to live in this little backwards, country town, stuck in the middle of nowhere?" asked Mr. Jones.

"It's the only place I could find a job. After my divorce, I went back to school to study physical therapy because I've always loved helping people. When I graduated I wanted a fresh start—but also wanted to live close to family. My Aunt Vicky invited me to stay with her until I could get on my feet."

Mr. Jones added, "I understand you wanting to be near family. And you come from a good family. Yes indeed." He clicked the mouse again.
 "Well, it's about time this site came up."

"I admit there are other places I could've moved to. But I love this area and being near the coast. After having spent all those years in the city with my ex-husband, I wanted to live in a nice little town. We used to come here all the time to visit my family and I always appreciated the warmth of the people. Most of all being here just feels right—like this is where I belong. And until today, I never questioned my decision to move to Solstice."

Mr. Jones peered over his glasses, listening to Marcella, taking in her insightful observations. "Hmm, I see. Well, if it feels right then you're most likely in the right place. Come here, I want to show you something. You too, Bill."

Bill Fletcher listened intently to Mr. Jones relay the rest of his story to Marcella. Having worked with Reggie Jones for the past twenty odd years, he'd already experienced the *pleasure* of hearing Papa Leroy's predictions of his great-grandson's magnificent future and the demise of mankind. Heard it too many times to count. As far as he was concerned, the principal was just as loony as his Papa Leroy. In fact, in all his forty years of living in Solstice, he never came across anyone he believed was put there by angels. He was a bonafide skeptic and didn't care who knew.

Even Bill's wife got on his nerves with all that Oya mumbo-jumbo. Always talking about how special someone's child was. *"Oo wee, he's definitely an Oya. Look at his eyes. That child has the eyes of an old soul,"* or *"Bill, do you think I'm an Oya? Small children and animals seem to love me so much."* When she got like that, Bill politely nodded and ignored her until she quieted down.

"This is something I came across a while ago. At the beginning of the year, every school in the district has to assemble a separate report to submit to the school board for their annual report. This spreadsheet lists all students by their student ID number, address, and date of birth. I thought I'd made a mistake, so I ran the report several times. Take a look, the information is correct." He removed his glasses, rubbing the weariness from his face.

Stud ID	Name	Address	DOB
11101	Jerald Masters	41101 Hightower	11 Jan
11110	Johan Grate	10011 Windy Dr	1 Jan
11111	Summer Daye	12111 Haven St	1 Nov
11112	Crystal Glass	1113 Weston Cir	1 Jan
11113	Devine Peake	70111 Anskon	11 Nov
11114	Jesus Islord	111 Lowell Ave	11 Jan
11115	Autumn Knight	41111 Gateway	11 Nov
11116	Windy Raine	1118 Rainbow Way	1 Nov
11117	Moses Walker	1110 Mountain Rd	11 Jan
11118	Precious Lorde	5111 Lakeview	1 Nov
11119	Gabrielle Angel	3111 Welcome Ave	11 Nov
11120	Archie Angel	3111 Welcome Ave	11 Nov

"Mr. Jones, how can this be? Both fifth grade classes are filled with students whose birthdays fall on January 1, January 11, November 1, and November 11. According to your report, half of the students have already turned 11; the rest will turn 11 later in the school year. Wow, that's even more bizarre! Look at their addresses—even the student ID numbers include multiple ones! What is that about? Is it some kind of anomaly—a coincidence?!" Marcella felt a hot ball of fire growing in the pit of her belly. The warmth spread to her limbs and out to her fingertips. A veil of blackness crossed her vision and she became lightheaded.

Bill caught Marcella just before she hit the floor and eased her into a chair. Mr. Jones pulled a bottle of water from his office refrigerator, tipped her head back and rubbed the cool bottle against her forehead. Bill fanned her with a manila folder.

"Miss Butler, are you okay? Marcella! Marcella, wake up!" Bill shook her gently.

"What happened?" She slowly sat upright, gaining her bearings.

"You fainted. Are you all right?" Mr. Jones asked, returning to his seat.

"Yeah, yeah I'm okay. Guess I got a bit spooked for a minute, that's all," she stammered.

"Spooked? Spooked about what?" asked Bill, returning to the chair opposite hers.

"Um, well, uh… for one thing my birthday is October 11th. I was born at 1:11 in the morning. And the house I rented a month ago is on NW 111th Street." Marcella shifted her focus between the principal and Fletcher.

"Tell you something else. All my life, I've noticed the number eleven. I see it everywhere. On billboards, in addresses, in advertisements, on license plates, on digital displays. I know I probably sound crazy, but it's almost as if I'm drawn to the number one, eleven, and one hundred and eleven." She gulped water from the bottle used to cool her forehead. "I wrote it off as coincidence and tried to convince myself that I only noticed it because I tried so hard not to. Never told anyone this before….."

"Interesting. Very interesting…. What else have you noticed that seems out of the ordinary? Anyone ever describe you as being strange or unusual? Different? You ever feel like you were out-of-step with the average person? That you marched to a beat only you could hear?" asked, the principal, hoping to find out who Marcella was.

"Since you asked, my ex-husband used to teasingly refer to me as "Lady Dr Phil" because so many people sought out my advice. One time a fortune teller said my aura was light, airy, refined, and heavenly. She called me ethereal. I never saw it, but many others have."

In hindsight, Marcella reflected on how she had lived her life. Always the first in line to help others, she usually put their needs above her own. It was one of the reasons her husband divorced her. Said she would give away her heart if someone asked for it.

"Hmm, that's interesting." Mr. Jones repeated again. "Perhaps this is a coincidence, because I've experienced much of what you have. My birthday is January 11 and I also am drawn to the number 1 or 11." He checked the time. "We should be heading back soon"

Marcella added, "I don't know if this means anything, but I also think I have premonitions. I often know what's going to happen before it actually does. I've thought about people I haven't heard from in years, when totally out of the blue, I'll get an email or phone call. Some call it self-fulfilling prophecies. You think something is going to happen, so you subconsciously make it happen. Others call it coincidence."

Bill Fletcher snorted, "Jiminy Cricket! What's with all this crazy talk? You're not any more special that I am! Neither one of you!" He threw his hands in the air.

Marcella ignored his comment and focused on Mr. Jones. "I've always been a bit different, kind of quirky, so I never put much thought into it until now." She stifled a yawn, trying to get oxygen to her tired brain. "What are you getting at? You think I'm one of the *Chosen Ones*—an Oya?"

"Well, let me show you this website I found…" said Mr. Jones.

Before he could go further, a strong gust of wind suddenly made its way down the center hallway, scattering children's artwork into the office. The howling wind grew louder with the passing of each second. Whatever storm brewed in the distance was now directly overhead. The light momentarily flickered then went completely dark. The computer also lost power. They stopped speaking and looked at one another, wondering what to do next. Each saw the terror they felt inside displayed on the other's face.

"There was no way the wind could have gotten inside. We made certain every door and window was locked. Didn't we?" Mr. Jones asked the other two. He shrugged off his suit jacket, trying hard not to make a sound.

"Yeah, I think so. What a minute. Shit! Are you telling me we didn't check the cafeteria? The largest room in the school and we forgot to check it?" Bill slapped his forehead.

"That's not possible, we covered every inch of this building!" exclaimed Mr. Jones.

"I'm going to take a look. Be right back." Bill Fletcher pretended he wasn't afraid and he definitely wasn't going to let a little thunderstorm scare him. If Jones wanted to be a wimp and run to the basement and hide like a little girl, well, that was on him.

Marcella and the principal remained crouched behind the desk, listening for anything out of the ordinary. Other than the drone of the wind, the school was eerily quiet. They watched Bill slink from the room doing his best imitation of a cat burglar.

Fletcher kept his back close to the wall, making his way slowly towards the direction of the gusting wind. Though he didn't believe that supernatural forces were at work, he didn't want to take any chances. After all, he wasn't a total fool. He'd been around long enough to hear the stories.

The cafeteria was at the end of the hallway, around the corner—about 150 feet away. The windowless hallway offered no light to ease his journey. Once he turned the corner, he would no longer be able to see the office, and the noise from the wind would keep the others from hearing his calls for help. His heart pounded heavily and he wondered if whatever was out there could hear it too.

He was understandably nervous, but he wasn't afraid. He could just make out the light coming from the cafeteria. One of the cafeteria's heavy double doors slammed open and shut with each strong gust of wind. Paper debris flew past, littering the hallway and brushing against his body. Boom, boom, boom! The twin doors slammed first shut then open. As he got closer, the sound of glass breaking stopped him dead in his tracks. Adrenaline kicked in, causing his heart to beat even harder against his chest.

"I'm okay, I'm okay It's only the wind. Gotta calm down. Can't let that man's foolish talk frighten me," he said quietly to himself. "I'll go in, shut the window and be out in no time."

Bill inched his way closer to the cafeteria. His feet were heavy as lead as each step closed the gap between him and the unknown. The wind howled, getting louder and stronger. "Gotta keep my cool. It's only the wind, only a storm, nothing to be afraid of."

Bill felt droplets of moisture from the rushing wind. He hugged closer to the wall, trying to stay out of the way of the heavy door. He managed to grab a hold of one of the door handles and looked inside. "Holy shit! What the hell?!" he screamed.

CHAPTER 3

Marcella and Principal Jones remained hidden in the confines of the office space. Darkness rapidly settled around them, filling the space with ever changing sinewy shadows. Vivid imaginations and stories filled with town folk's superstitions only added to the stress of waiting for Bill Fletcher to return. They listened and waited for the howling wind to subside; notifying them that Bill had succeeded. So far, nothing had changed. The wind continued to sweep through the building. It may not have been the best idea for him to go alone, but someone had to stay hang back to bring word to the teachers and children that the school was secure.

The last thing either of them wanted was for one of the other teachers to leave the kids behind.

"We should probably be getting back to the children." Mr. Jones looked at his watch. "We've been gone too long already. Where the hell is Fletcher?"

"Yeah, you're right," Marcella peeked around the desk into the hallway. "But we've got to wait for Bill to get back. He should be there by now. Give him time, there's no telling what he's dealing with there."

"I'll give him a few more minutes. If he's not back, we'll go looking for him. We've got to make sure this building is secure before heading back down. God only knows what will make its way inside if a window or door is carelessly left open." The last statement was made more for his sake than anyone else's.

"Mr. Jones, before... well, you were saying," Marcella cleared her throat. "Uh, you mentioned or you alluded that maybe I could be an Oya? You were also about to show me something on the internet before the computer went down. Tell me what's going on!"

He sighed heavily, "Alright, I'll try to explain. I wanted to show you a website dedicated to people who believe they have been chosen by angels. When I was a little boy, Papa Leroy explained to me that there are spirits who walk amongst the ordinary. Solstice is, and for as long as I can remember, has been a safe haven for these folks. Marcella, there are millions of people all over the world—from all walks of life, all religions, all races, who have been chosen to help make this world the one God intended it to be. After seeing how humans turned out, guess he figured we needed a little help from above." He hesitated and listened for any strange noises from the hallway.

"It sounds unbelievable, but certain people experience a phenomenon with an unusual connection to the prompt of 1:11 or 11:11. The only thing these people have in common is that they are connected by the number one. We believe this phenomenon is a wake-up call for us to become engaged in fighting the battle against evil. The angels use these prompts, if you will, to wake people up to get in touch with their spirituality. He wants these people, the Oya, to go out and spread goodness, and help others to live their best lives—in peace, in harmony, by loving one another." He stopped speaking for a moment to listen.

"Chosen ones don't belong to any particular group. Some Oya stumble upon each other by accident, others out of curiosity due to a sudden obsession with the number one or eleven. You wouldn't believe how easy it is to find this information on the internet..." he chuckled. "Oya were put here to remind people not to squander their lives—to touch others and to spread a message of Love. Are you with me so far?"

"Yeah, I mean yes, please go on."

"Unfortunately, there is a flip side."

"There usually is."

"There's a flip side because evil lives on in man. According to stories passed down from slaves who settled this land, evil creatures have been searching for this town since the beginning of time. Their only mission is to destroy this world as we know it by spreading hate and fear.

They divide men and emphasize our differences rather than bring us together. These creatures spread evil through any means necessary: schools, rallies, radio, television, and especially the internet."

"The town of Solstice has been able to remain undetected until now. For centuries it was considered to be a safe haven for Oya, but we are by no means the only town to provide a refuge. These enclaves exist throughout the world," he sighed wearily.

"So the Oya in Solstice aren't the only ones?"

"Heavens no! They are—I mean, we are everywhere. And just as Oya are chosen by the Creator, the evil ones belong to the devil. He puts them here to destroy, to seek out the Oya and take over the souls of men. The dark forces are determined and will stop at nothing. Nothing!"

"Mr. Jones, I believe in God, but I don't know if I believe in *Chosen* people, or so called angels who get wake-up calls from digital alarm clocks. Yeah, I know there are very, very bad people out there, but to say that they are taken over by evil forces… Like it's some great battle of good against evil?! It all sounds so, so friggin' ridiculous!" She attempted to poke holes in his logic. Otherwise his explanation meant the end of the world may be at hand.

"I understand your skepticism, Marcella. Trust me, I was once a skeptic too. But I've seen evil in action, especially over the past few years. This country is now more divided than ever! Sometimes, it seems that the evil ones are winning." He wiped his brow and continued.

"I started seeing 111 prompts just a few years ago. Now the string of 1's appear when I least expect them. I see that number at the grocery store, on taxi cabs, phone numbers, on my computer clock, but the school report is what really shook me up. I began researching the phenomena shortly thereafter."

Marcella asked, "Suppose what you're saying is true? What happens if the Oya, the ones who see 111, don't act on the prompt? Suppose they decide to live a life *not* filled with goodness? Maybe they don't see this *calling* as a blessing. What if they succumb to temptations of evil? Then what?"

"I don't claim to be an expert, but I can't imagine Oyas not living a spiritual life. It goes against reasoning because it's embedded in their DNA to be good. To do the right thing, even when everything around them says otherwise. I'm not saying they're perfect people, but they are *chosen*. Plain and simple. Oya can be preachers, counselors, teachers, social directors, foster parents, nurses.... They are also poets,

OYA - THE CHOSEN ONES

entertainers, writers, musicians, actors, artists, cooks, etc. The list goes on and on. Oya can be anyone, but not just anyone can be an Oya. You get my point?"

"Yes, I think I do. Looking back on my life, I suppose I have lived a *different* sort of life." Marcella shook her head over and over. "Huh, ain't that something?! Growing up, my brothers and sisters used to call me Miss Goody Two-Shoes. My husband hated that I was always trying to help folks. He said it like it was a bad thing. Mr. Jones, I've always known in my heart that I was put here to do something more. Just didn't know what it was. Thought I was being arrogant," she sighed.

"Unfortunately most people will always question your motives."

"I started seeing multiple ones about the time I got married—about 10 years ago. Saw those numbers practically everywhere. I tried to ignore it, but the more I did, the more frequent it became. I thought I was losing my mind and becoming obsessed with numbers. You remember that Russell Crowe movie, *A Beautiful Mind* and that other one with Jim Carrey, *The Number 23*? I was afraid to tell anyone about my obsession. Thought I was going nuts!"

"No, you're not crazy. But you must understand what we're up against, because the elders from long ago knew this day would come. Up until now, the evil creatures have laid low. Only doing enough to stir up trouble for the Oya. According to the stories my great-grandfather told me, a whole other kind of evil has been unleashed today." He looked around the corner again.

"Papa Leroy said the day would come when evil forces would make themselves known and come to finish off what the old devil started long ago. The creatures come from another dimension. They are older than time and live in that space none of us can see. Unable to be detected, they get under people's skin and plant evil thoughts into their minds causing utter chaos. Some people go insane because unfortunately, they have the ability to see the demons all the time."

Marcella slowly took in his words. She reluctantly allowed the images to sink into her consciousness. She needed to understand what she was up against. Good versus evil? *Chosen ones—Oyas,* placed in Solstice and other safe havens around the world? Oya being sought out by demons on a mission to destroy them?

An instinctive and protective maternal instinct kicked in for her students. Waiting in the basement of the small elementary school was a room filled with innocent young children— including young Oya patiently awaiting their call to action. It was up to them to stop the world from being destroyed!

CHAPTER 4

Bill Fletcher watched in awe. Or perhaps, shock, as he took in the spectacle unfolding before him. Jerald, the little boy from the soccer field, stood in the middle of a mass of swirling images. The images shifted from dark shadows to town's people he recognized and surrounded the child. Jerald was caught in the vortex of a growing tornado. Many images appeared to be human shaped, while others resembled something from a nightmare. Despite the chaos, Jerald firmly stood his ground. Immovable in the face of disaster, in the midst of the storm, he never lost his composure.

With head held back and eyes closed tightly, Jerald stretched both arms upwards. The boy's lips moved, but the earsplitting noises covered their meaning. Taking a closer look, Bill Fletcher thought his eyes were playing tricks on him, for it appeared the child's finger tips were translucent. Like they were illuminated from the inside by an invisible light. He blinked several times to clear his vision, yet nothing changed.

From a small open window high above the lunch tables, Bill watched as dark clouds found their way inside, joining and strengthening the growing vortex. The sound of the howling wind was deafening. Debris struck his body almost knocking Bill from his feet. He stumbled, which was enough motion to cause attention to his presence. The dark images drifted closer and he tried to scream, but no sound escaped from his throat. The air drained from Bill's lungs as the first shadowy images stopped mere inches from his face. Looking directly into the face of the devil, he didn't move an inch. The demon opened its mouth and snarled, releasing a noxious ancient fume of death into the room.

As Bill opened his mouth to scream again, the demon swiftly shot what appeared to be a shadowy plume of smoke into Bill's mouth and down his throat.

Bill Fletcher involuntarily inhaled the vapor, choking on the vile substance as it spread throughout his body and attached itself to his every cell. He doubled over in agony trying to vomit up the devil's seed, but it was too late, for he'd already succumbed to the demon's spell. The cunning demon buried itself deep into his subconscious and would only make his appearance known when necessary. To the normal person, Bill appeared, well—normal.

Several minutes passed before he was finally able to relax. Now filled with the spirit's evil intentions, he stood to his feet and carefully inched backwards towards the door, all the while keeping an eye on Jerald. The vortex continued to grow larger, feeding itself from dark spirits which continued to enter through the window.

Bill was almost out the door when all of a sudden Jerald dropped his head ever so slightly, opened his eyes and shouted, "Wait! Need Oya! Get the other children! Now!"

In the natural, Bill Fletcher had no idea what Jerald meant. He stumbled from the cafeteria and locked the doors behind him. He felt guilty leaving Jerald alone, but there was nothing he could do to help.

Unable to catch his breath, he was on the verge of hyperventilating. *Oh shit! Oh shit! What the fuck was that? I must be losing my mind! What was he trying to tell me?* He rubbed his eyes, finally able to breathe again. But each time he inhaled, he felt a sharp stabbing pain in his chest.

Those things! Those shadows! Jerald! What the hell is going on? With his back against the wall, Bill sank to the floor, trying to pull himself together. He continued to watch the door, fully aware of what was taking place on the other side. Subconsciously he thought over and over again, *I must bring back the Oya. Bring back the Oya.*

* * *

"Bill's been gone way too long. I've got to go find him. I knew I shouldn't have let him go alone."

"Mr. Jones, the cafeteria *is* only around the corner." She stopped speaking. "Hey listen, the wind has stopped. Well, I guess old Bill took care of the job just like he said he would." *Maybe he's not so bad after all.* Marcella felt she owed Bill an apology for how she treated him earlier.

"Are you alright to walk? Still feeling lightheaded?" He offered his hand to Marcella stand.

"I'm fine. I feel much better now. Let's go."

"Please call me Reggie. After today, I think you've earned it."

"Alright, Reggie it is. But you're still Mr. Jones in front of the children."

Minus the ever present noise of the wind, the silence was quite deafening. Marcella and Mr. Jones crept down the hallway and headed towards the cafeteria. It was almost completely dark in this part of the school. Turning the corner, they heard him before they saw him. Bill Fletcher sat against the wall, head between his knees, laughing uncontrollably. He looked as if he were hysterical.

"Bill? Hey Bill? Yo?! What's going on man? You alright?" Mr. Jones whispered loudly.

Bill looked up upon hearing his boss's voice.

At the sight of the two Oya, the demon almost made its presence known. However, it was clever and understood these two would lead it directly to the others. He quickly stood and wiped the tears from his face. Nervously looking behind him towards the closed doors, Bill headed in their direction.

"Shhh, quiet! Don't say another word! I've got to get you two out of here! I must bring the other Oya!" he stated in a monotone voice, staring off blankly into space.

"What's wrong man? You okay? You closed the window, right?" asked Mr. Jones. Something wasn't right. Bill didn't seem like his usual self. He seemed slightly off.

"Shhh! I said be quiet! You can't let them know you're here. It's not safe. Let's get back downstairs with the others and I'll tell you everything." Bill rushed past them and motioned for them to follow.

The two practically ran to the basement, trying to keep up with Bill in the lead. Through the long dark narrow hallway and down two flights of stairs, they didn't stop until they were outside the storage room. Fear, physical exertion, and adrenaline flooding through their veins, left all three out of breath.

"Bill, you want to fill us in on what happened up there? You're as white as a ghost!" Mr. Jones removed his tie and rolled up his shirt sleeves.

"Yeah, okay. You might not believe me, but..." He described what had occurred from the time he left the office until they found him sitting in the hallway. The demon rose to the surface of Bill's consciousness prepared to pounce at a moment's notice.

"So what do we do now? What did Jerald mean? What was he trying to tell you?" asked Marcella.

"It means we need to act fast!" Mr. Jones declared. "Wow! That's incredible! Jerald is holding them off as we speak? Alone?"

"Yeah, it does almost unbelievable… But if what Bill Fletcher said is true, we don't have much time. We have to help Jerald."

"Let's get the adults together first. I want to be sure we're doing the right thing. Liz will know what to do. Listen, before we go inside, let's compose ourselves. I don't want to frighten the children anymore than they already are. Agreed? Marcella, are you up for this?"

"Do I have a choice?" She tightened her ponytail in preparation for what may become the fight of her life.

Mr. Jones knocked. Mrs. Hernandez released the bolt lock and slowly opened the door. It was stuffy inside, as hundreds of sweaty kids did not make for a refreshing greeting. Liz and the older children were serving punch and cookies to the little ones. The aides were organizing several classes into putting on an impromptu play—

anything to keep them calm. The generator hummed steadily along, providing light and powering a fan to circulate the stale air.

"Hello children. We're back! Pretty soon, you'll be out of here and back with your parents in no time at all. But first, I want to play a little game. When I call your name, I want you to follow Miss Liz into the front of the room. Only go if your name is called. Okay?" Mr. Jones wanted to hurry, but didn't want to frighten the other children.

He retrieved a sheet of paper from his pants pocket. Before shutting the computer down, he printed the list of students they suspected were Oya. "If your name isn't called, I want you to wait with Miss Hernandez's group towards the back. It's very important that we get this correct. Okay? He smiled as he called out the very unique names. "Autumn Knight, Summer Daye, Crystal Glass, Devon Peake, Jonah Grate…."

The students waited patiently listening for their names to be called. Five minutes and 28 children later, they gathered into their group. All were thought to be Oya—*the Chosen Ones*. To look at them, they were not remarkable or special. In fact, they were anything but. They looked to be average kids in every way that mattered. The Rainbow Coalition would be proud, for the children represented a cross section of society, despite the town being predominantly African-American.

"Alright children, listen up. I need to talk to you about something very important." Liz's soft spoken, grandmotherly voice was reassuring. They trusted her. "How many of your parents have told you how special you are?"

All twenty-eight of the children's hands shot up simultaneously. However, one of the younger looking eleven year olds kept an eye on Mr. Fletcher. He was in the corner talking to himself and acting really weird. The little girl watching Fletcher had always been taught to respect her elders, including her teacher, so she didn't say anything. Just kept watching.

"Good. That's very good, because every single one of you is very, very, special. You were born with a prophetic gift that some bad people want to take away. But we're not going to let that happen." She pointed to Mr. Jones and Marcella. "In fact, we're special too."

"Miss Liz, my father said that one day evil spirits might come and try to make my friends do bad things, but it's up to me to help them be good. Right?" The girl glanced backwards at Mr. Fletcher.

"That's exactly right Crystal. Well, it's time for all of us to use our good to fight against the evil creatures. It might seem scary at first, but trust me you are not alone. We have help from a higher power and this is how you will receive your energy. I want you to do exactly what I'm doing now." She threw her head back and raised both arms up as high as she could. Stretched her hands so her fingertips would literally connect with the Almighty.

"Hey, I know how to do that. It's easy! Look, I can do it!" remarked another girl standing towards the front.

"That's exactly what you need to do. We've got to go help Jerald now because he really needs our help. He's alone trying to fight off the bad spirits all by himself. He asked Mr. Fletcher to gather you to help him out." She continued to smile as she relayed instructions.

"That's right children, pay close attention to Miss Liz because we have to go in very, very soon." Mr. Jones stated, staring at the door.

"You may see these things shift into hideous shapes of monsters and demons, but I don't want you to be frightened. These evil spirits are afraid of us, especially you children. You have a special name we call you—Oya. You can conjure up the elements to help you fight these things and send them back to hell where they belong." She paused to allow the revelation sink into their young, yet very mature minds.

"A long time ago, freed slaves looking for a better life resettled in this town. They immediately knew this was a special place with special people. So they started calling those people Oya. Oyas are warriors of wind, lightning, fire and magic. They are thought to create hurricanes and tornadoes and keep evil from settling in our world. You children were sent here especially to plant seeds of love, joy, and peace in everyone you come in contact with." Liz continued.

"They see your goodness and want to take it, but they don't know how. If we all work together, we can send the evil creatures back to where they came from. Are you guys ready?" She scanned the group.

"Yes ma'am, we're ready. Let's go get those evil spirits! Let's go help Jerald!" A chorus of voices expressed their sentiment. They jumped up and down excitedly, as only children would do at a time like this.

"What about him? Mr. Fletcher? Is he one too?" Crystal picked up bad vibes coming from her teacher standing in the corner talking to himself.

Liz wondered what kind of evil Fletcher saw that could turn him into a bumbling idiot. He stood with his back to the group mumbling incoherently and gesturing like a madman. She wanted to distance the Oya from him because he acted as if he on the verge of losing it. Without knowing what was wrong, there was no way to offer assistance. Unfortunately, Fletcher would have to wait. They didn't have the time to deal with him.

CHAPTER 5

Principal Jones and Marcella led the rag tag group towards their destiny. Bill Fletcher and Liz brought up the rear. The children transformed into serious little adults, focused on the mission at hand. As quiet as ninjas, the pint sized warriors crept silently through the school, as if they instinctively knew what awaited them.

Within minutes, the group stood outside the cafeteria watching the doors shake as if something were trying to get out. The Oya heard the roar of the wind on the other side, but they were not frightened. In fact, a look of quiet determination was evident on everyone's face, except for Bill's. Bill Fletcher was never an Oya, this they all understood.

"Mr. Jones, I think I may have made a mistake. I'm not one of you. I shouldn't be here. I'm not an Oya. In fact, I think the only reason these creatures let me go was to lure the children to them. Oh my God! What have I done?" He backed away from the group.

"Bill, calm yourself man! You've done nothing wrong. It doesn't matter how the children got here. What matters is that they're here now. We Oya are not supposed to hide from these creatures! The Oya were put here to battle evil head on and that's exactly what we're going to do. You're not safe with us. Go back to the basement. Miss Hernandez and the other teachers need you with them."

"But, but, w-w-what shall I tell them? How will I know when it's over? When it's safe?" He nervously watched the door shake, threatening to burst open at any moment.

The group watched in horror as Bill Fletcher's body began to involuntarily shake. His eyes rolled back into his head until only the whites showed. A dark foul smelling smoke poured from his every orifice and funky green mucus spilled from his mouth. The demon pushed forth and shook itself free from Bill's body, leaving him lying on the floor like a discarded bag of trash. It rose up and roared at the group of children.

The demon swooped down over the group of Oya and howled loudly, surveying its opponent. The children instinctively assumed a battle stance in preparation for an attack. The demon saw the group of Oya was too powerful to tackle on its own, so it rejoined forces with the vortex of evil forming in the cafeteria.

Mr. Jones carefully approached and stooped over Bill Fletcher's lifeless body. He shook his head in pity and whispered, "I'm sorry man. You didn't deserve to go out like that!" He turned to face his small army and prayed he was making the right decision. His heart told him they were doing the right thing.

Marcella, Liz and the children surrounded Bill's body and said a quick prayer. If that thing was powerful enough to do that to Bill, there was no telling what else it would do to them.

"Children, when I open this door, you'll see and hear things that may frighten you. However, I know your parents have prepared you for this day. You are protected because you were chosen by God's angels themselves. These evil creatures cannot hurt you if you stand strong together. Jerald is in there all by himself, he's probably really tired so we need to get in there to help him. Does anyone have questions?" explained Mr. Jones. The doors shook more violently than ever.

"Miss Butler, are you and Miss Liz also Oya? Will you be there with us?" asked a little boy with huge brown eyes.

Both women looked at the other, nodded in synch, and smiled at themselves and the children. They grabbed one of Bill's arms and moved his body to a corner.

Marcella felt badly for Bill Fletcher. He wasn't a bad guy and it was too bad the evil spirit got inside him. She held his hand and prayed his soul would be at rest. As she was finishing her prayer, she dropped his hand and shouted in surprise, "Guys, Bill's alive! He moved his fingers."

"That's wonderful news Marcella! Uh, forgive me, because I don't mean to sound insensitive, but we have a war to fight. If Bill is the fighter I know him to be, he'll be just fine. We're running out of time. Are you ready to go?!" Liz gently pulled her away.

"I'm ready if you are," Marcella answered.

Mr. Jones struggled with the heavy doors. With Marcella and Liz's help, he pulled it open. The door slammed against the wall, knocking him backwards. Marcella broke his fall.

Jerald stood in the center of what was once the cafeteria. The roof was gone, leaving the child exposed to the elements. The wind whipped around debris until it resembled a huge tornado. Inside the vortex wall, shadowy figures surrounded the child in a mass of swirling darkness. The group watched shadows shift into demonic forms attempting to make Jerald falter. He could not be moved.

The Oya children approached the storm that threatened to destroy their brother—their friend, and everyone they knew, yet they were not afraid. Unexpectedly, the mass began to break apart. A horrendous and excruciatingly loud growling noise reverberated throughout the shadowy vortex with each step the group took.

Dark masses continuously swooped down upon the children trying to frighten them, but they stood fast in their determination. The Oya joined hands and continued forward. All 28 children and 3 adults walked though the wall of that vortex and surrounded Jerald to form a protective barrier around him.

Jerald opened his eyes and exclaimed, "Oya, protectors of all that is good and pure! Send these demons back to the hell from where they came! You do not belong here! Your evil is not welcome! Back to hell demons! Oya! Our time has come! Let them know they will not win!" he shouted at the top of his lungs.

The children dropped hands and stretched their arms upwards to the sky. The ground rumbled beneath their feet, the sun's rays broke through the dark clouds and reached down towards the children's outstretched fingers.

The demonic shadows grew angrier with this new attack. They became emboldened, throwing objects at the children, and displaying disfigured faces of loved ones—anything to distract the Oya, to scare them, to make them run and hide. Nothing worked. The more destruction the creatures initiated, the stronger the group's force became.

Mr. Jones watched the young Oya in action. The children called upon their inner spirits to join with the divine creator to form a powerful force. They absorbed the energy and reflected back the bright light, becoming almost translucent in the process. With great intensity, they battled the evil lurking in the shadows surrounding their small bodies.

The demons gathered strength and tossed a few of the children outside. Realizing it was easier to fight the Oya on an individual basis, they picked the group apart, one-by-one.

"Liz! Marcella! Get the ones going after the children! They're trying to break up the group!" shouted Mr. Jones above the noise.

Liz and Marcella went toe to toe with the demonic creatures shooting from the vortex, making individual attacks. It seemed like it wasn't enough. The more they fought them off, the stronger the dark forces became. Mr. Jones made it his mission to return the fragile children to the group as quickly as the darkness slung them away.

Movement in the school's hallway caught his eye. It was Bill Fletcher! He weakly limped into the cafeteria holding his wounds together, having led the rest of the faculty and students to battle the demons. Over a hundred students and teachers charged towards the creatures, yelling and screaming as if noise alone would do the trick.

The remaining children fought their way through gaps in the vortex wall, enforcing the protective barrier provided by the Oya. The adults did the same. Many were hit by debris— some very serious, but none gave up. They took their place behind the Oya and joined hands encircling the group. Everyone who could began to pray loudly. This made the evil demonic creatures furious, but it started to work.

One by one, the shadowy masses retreated back into the dark clouds, until only the swirling wind remained. A tremendous sonic boom vibrated throughout the air. And as quickly as it all began, it was over. It was finally over.

As if coming out of a trance, the young Oya dropped their arms, opened their eyes, and surveyed the destruction. The remaining children and adults did the same. Remnants of a tornado hitting the school were evident everywhere and the entire cafeteria and top floor of the school were destroyed. Cars were tossed around like toys in the field where the class played soccer earlier.

Children were scratched up, a few even had broken bones, but none were seriously injured. And just like that, they became kids again. Talking, laughing, and replaying the day's events, they were understandably excited. And realizing what they had accomplished, they were amazed at what they'd done.

"Hey Bill. Thank you for everything. You know we couldn't have done this without your help." Marcella brushed dirt from his shirt. "How did you know?"

"I didn't know, not really. After watching Jerald hold those creatures off by himself and then seeing your group join in to help, I figured it couldn't hurt to have everyone work together to get rid of those things. I had to do something once I realized I had a second chance. Thought I was a goner…"

"Yeah, we thought we'd lost you," said Marcella.

"But when I saw what you all were up against, I pulled myself together and somehow made it down to the basement. Don't know how I made it," he remarked.

"I'm glad you made it," added Mr. Jones offered his hand in friendship.

"You know what they say, it takes a village!" Bill Fletched accepted his grasp.

"You're absolutely right Mr. Fletcher! It does take a village. And today, it took everyone in this school working together to protect this town, and possibly the world as we know it. I have no doubt they will be back, but I am more confident than ever they will not win. Not on my watch!" Liz slapped him a high five.

"Jerald you did a great job today! We're all so proud of you. And I'm sure your parents will be even more proud once I tell him what you did. You were so brave. Weren't you afraid?"

"No, Mr. Jones, I wasn't scared at all. When I was around 5, my parents told me about the Oya. About how we were put here to protect others from evil. I used to see scary monsters when I was younger. They used to hide in our house and really scare me. When I told my parents, they told me to not be afraid because the monsters could only hurt me if I gave them power. So I learned to ignore them as if they weren't there. After that, they didn't scare me anymore. Today, when I heard that loud sound and saw them in the cafeteria, I knew God would protect me and He did."

"You're right son, He certainly did." Mr. Jones hugged the boy close in a fatherly embrace.

After that day, the townspeople of Solstice went on with life as if nothing happened. When outsiders asked about the sonic boom, the earthquake, and a tornado all in one day, they replied that it was probably a freak storm—an anomaly.

When all was said and done, life for the Oya returned to normal and they went back to living their lives waiting for the next attack. They had won the battle, but the war still raged.

Bill Fletcher continued teaching music. Marcella Butler opened her own physical therapy clinic and hired Liz as a part-time receptionist.

Mr. Jones continued to excel as principal, leading Smith Elementary school's fifth grade class to receive the highest scores in the state on the aptitude test. And Jerald went on to middle school, tutoring younger students in reading when he wasn't on the field playing kickball.

THE END

About the Author

Patricia Hopkins is originally from St. Louis, Missouri. She rediscovered her love of writing after publishing her first novel, *More Than A Notion*. When she's not writing, she's in the kitchen whipping up exotic dishes or baking homemade cupcakes. She currently lives in Virginia with her family.

Coming soon, *"Living In The Offbeat"*.